# DESPERATE HOUSEWIVES OF AVALON

SARANNA DEWYLDE

Corvus Coron

Published in the United States of America by

Saranna DeWylde © 2014, 2023

Cover Art by Dee J Holmes

ISBN 13: 978-1-948001-32-8 (ebook)

978-1-948001-30-4 (print)

# CHAPTER
# ONE

ARTEMIS

"I didn't wrap your gift," Aphrodite said around a mouthful of lamb pizza.

Artemis was already wary. First, Aphrodite had invited her out to Pomegranate Pizza and she *never* dined out on Ambrosia Lane. Even for special occasions like her birthday. She preferred the mortal world and Brooklyn Style pizza to Cyclops-tossed crust. Aphrodite even made her a dark chocolate, caramel, and sea salt birthday cake—with mocha frosting. Aphrodite hated baking.

Artemis was sure this present was going to be a doozy of cataclysmic proportions. "What is it?" Artemis eyed her like she would a Japanese Rhinoceros Beetle, rather than her best friend.

"You're making that face." Aphrodite took a drink of her sparkling red wine.

"What face?"

"Like you just stepped in a pile of Kraken poo."

"Well, they say Love stinks." Artemis wouldn't know, she'd never been in love. Although she took great joy in needling the other goddess.

"I do not!" Aphrodite made a big show of raising her arms and sniffing.

"You know what I mean. I adore you, but I'm suspicious of your gifts. I saw what you did to my brother and Nyx. I don't need *any* part of that." No, she didn't need it, but part of her wanted it. Artemis was tired of being the universe's oldest virgin.

"That wasn't me. That was Fate. After the debacle with Ares, I'm not allowed to act in Fate's stead anymore." Aphrodite's mouth tightened.

"Now who's making a face? You're going to get wrinkles."

"I am not! What a wretched thing to say." Aphrodite smoothed her skin with her fingers, as if that would stop the slow march of time. Not that her skin would ever show it anyway, but Aphrodite was a vain creature.

Although, Artemis grudgingly admitted her vanity was warranted. Aphrodite was beautiful by any standard.

"Since it's your birthday, I'll give you a pass. But color yourself lucky I didn't zap you in love with Hercules for a crack like that."

"Now you're just being mean." Artemis shuddered.

"I am, aren't I? He's such a dick." Aphrodite flashed a serene smile. "Anyway, back to the task at hand. It's official. You *are* the world's oldest virgin."

"Persephone—" she protested weakly.

"You know you're older than she is. So even when she was a card carrying member of the V-Club you were still the world's oldest virgin. Don't you think it's time to cash in your V-Card?"

She should have known that Aphrodite would see right through any of her protestations. It was time to face facts. "It's *been* time, girl. But everyone on Olympus takes that whole virgin goddess thing so seriously. Like if I get laid there will be some kind of apocalypse. It's not like I have a mother like Demeter threatening to smite and destroy, etc. and so forth."

"No. Just a brother who is like, you know, the sun and will burn their faces off?"

"He doesn't care what I do with my goddess parts." Artemis crossed her arms. At least, he shouldn't. She didn't give him too much grief about his god parts. She may have told Nyx not to hurt him, but that was standard familial don't break my brother's heart type speech. She didn't mention his godhood...er...parts. *Gross. Whatever.*

"History says otherwise, but right now he's too busy with Nyx and their Baby of Doom."

She narrowed her eyes. Ephie may have been a Baby of Doom—she was a titan, and her realm was nightmares— but that was still her niece.

"Hey, I didn't say it was a bad thing." Aphrodite placated her. "Just that it's keeping him busy. So, in the interest of cashing in said V-Card, pick a god. Any god. I'll take care of the rest."

"Any god? Any at all?" A slow smile curved her lips.

"*Any*."

"What about Ares?" Artemis couldn't held being contrary. She certainly didn't want any part of that god and his unruly, wandering war hammer.

It was Aphrodite's turn to narrow her eyes. "If that's really who you want, I'll make it happen."

SARANNA DEWYLDE

Even though Aphrodite looked like she was about to plot a murder, there was a sadness in her eyes and Artemis immediately felt guilty. "No, I'm just giving you grief."

"Really? Because I wouldn't even have to zap him. He'd be happy to take care of your V without any prodding."

"No, really. He's all yours, babe," Artemis promised, holding up her hands, as if to ward off the vision of the pillaging war god coming to claim her V.

"That's part of the problem."

"Oh, whatever. I saw that laser glare of death when I suggested him. You still love him." This wasn't news to Artemis, but Aphrodite kept trying to deny she loved the war god.

"We're not talking about me, Artie. We're talking about you."

"Sad lot that I am. I'm Goddess of the Hunt. I should be able to catch a man."

"While all of them want to be last, a lot of them are afraid to be first, because they think you'll expect them to be last, if that makes sense. It's a paradox, really." Aphrodite drummed her fingers on the table, having lost interest in her pizza.

"That's why I need a bad boy. Someone who isn't going to bother about all that. Someone who will take pride in 'despoiling' me." Oh yeah. Artemis decided she was ready to be pillaged, despoiled, and all of that stuff.

"Hmm. There's always Loki. He's so hot." Aphrodite licked her lips.

But Artemis didn't see the allure. "Didn't he do that thing where he turned into a horse and did horse things with..." She couldn't even finish the sentence.

"Eh." Aphrodite shrugged. "I don't know what that was about."

"He's on the no list."

"But he's hot. And *bad*."

"He might be a little too much for me to handle at this point in the game." She couldn't get past the horse thing.

"I know!" Aphrodite perked up, her smile glowing bright. "Ra!"

"No." Definitely not.

The other goddess's face fell like a spoiled soufflé. "Why not? He's perfect."

"He's a sun god. He looks too much like my brother." He'd even had the balls to ask her out once and she totally would have said yes if he hadn't been almost the spitting image of Apollo.

"Oh." She bit her lip. "What about Odin?"

"No, no and *hell no*. He'd think I was one of his Valkyries, bound to his every whim. No thank you." That was an international incident waiting to happen. Artemis would put up with his crap for exactly two point five never.

"I'm fresh out of ideas." Aphrodite shrugged and leaned back in her chair.

"No, you're just fresh."

"I am," Aphrodite agreed. "But that's not getting us anywhere."

"I don't know. Maybe I should just pick a mortal. The next man who prays to me gets it." Could she really do that? Maybe.

"You can't be serious?" Aphrodite pushed her pizza around on her plate a few more times.

"I don't know, why not?" She shrugged. "You had that game with the apples."

"It's not the same. You're going to remember this first time for eternity. It should at least be with someone who can match your stamina."

Artemis knew she was right. "Who else could we tap?"

Aphrodite giggled. "You said tap."

Artemis smirked. "I sure did. I will tap that ass. Or will my ass *be* tapped?"

"Let's not put the batteries ahead of the vibrator."

"Is that like don't put the cart before the horse?"

Aphrodite nodded. "But considering earlier Loki conversation..."

"Gotcha. What about Krishna? I kind of dig the blue." He was hot, but wasn't really a bad boy.

"He could work. But he's not angsty enough for you. What about Aeron? I've never met him, but he's welsh. They're very earthy, like you. He hangs out in Avalon." Aphrodite's eyes went wide. "*Avalon!*"

Aphrodite said it like she'd just found treasure. Artemis didn't make the connection. "What's so special about Avalon? I mean, yeah it's an immortal resort spot of sorts, but there's Atlantis. Or the Triangle. Or—"

"Only one of the greatest bastards known to history. Mordred, son of Morgan Le Fey and King Arthur. He brought down the mighty Camelot. He is a very dark and tortured type." Aphrodite nodded as she spoke.

Electric current hummed through her fingertips just thinking about it. "He'll do."

"And if he doesn't, there's always Aeron. He's the god of death, war, slaughter or something. I can't remember. But he gives good wood, or so I've heard."

"I think it's time for an extended vacation." Artemis grinned. Their plot had geared up to full steam.

"An island vacation. Avalon has some lovely beaches. They get satellite, but no cell coverage, what with being hidden in the mist and such." Aphrodite tapped her finger on her chin. "Morgan has a lovely little guest house. I'm sure she wouldn't mind if you stayed with her. In fact, I'll send her a golden apple to add to her collection."

"Wait, wait." Artemis held up her hands. She realized she'd agreed to this without even taking a look at the guy. What if he was missing his teeth and was cross-eyed?

"What?" Aphrodite harrumphed.

"What does he look like?"

"Besides tormented deliciousness?" Aphrodite waved her fingers through the air in a delicate dance and an image emerged in Artemis's champagne.

Tormented deliciousness was exactly what he looked like. Shoulder length raven black hair, hard-angled features, with a scowl that could hold its own with Hades or Thanatos. A flutter started low in her belly and spread out through her limbs like a thousand butterflies. He was *The One*.

"He's perfect. Absolutely perfect."

"Go pack. I'm going to email Morgan. If she says no, you can always stay at the resort, but it will be good to have Mom on your side. And easier access to Mordred."

"You could come with me, you know," Artemis invited.

"Oh, no. Ares is getting too big for his toga. He's in for a serious smiting."

"Don't you mean shagging?"

"Shut. Up. I do not." Aphrodite pursed her lips.

"Oh, please. It's been like this for the last five hundred years. He huffs, he puffs, and *you* blow *him* down and around." Artemis rolled her eyes.

"What can I say? The God of War is good with guns. Especially his love gun."

"Love gun? Really?" Artemis arched a brow.

Aphrodite kept her face a mask of innocence. "Shag stick? Velvet revolver? Manroot? Bang bong?"

The looked at each other before cackling in unison, "Purple-headed womb ferret."

"Oh honey, you're going to have such a wonderful time." Aphrodite sighed. "I remember my first time. The chase is never quite the same. A word of warning though. Don't go falling in love with Mordred. He is the baddest of the bad and will break your heart."

"Puh-lease. This is about getting my card punched, which has nothing to do with my heart."

"Okay, I'll come to your temple after I hear back from Morgan and we'll do some shopping before you go."

The hurricane known as Artemis was about to make landfall in Avalon.

# TWO

GWEN

Guinevere du Lac decided while staring at the back of her husband's head that Happily Ever After was actually a big, fat, lie. She preferred the way the stories said she ended her days: in a convent repenting her sins. That she and golden boy never got together after the whole burning at the stake fiasco and that they'd never followed Arthur to Avalon and immortality. Not that she thought she had any sins to repent.

Some days she wondered if burning at the stake would have been better than spending eternity with Lance.

Just looking at him pissed her off. The way he breathed made her angry, especially when he was sleeping. Sometimes, she woke up at night and would roll over and look at him, cradled in his peaceful slumber, and wonder how he could just lay there and sleep when she was so unhappy.

His soft snores had once been endearing. Now, she'd pinch his nose closed so he'd wake up and roll over.

What she really hated was the fact his boxer briefs

never made it all the way into the laundry basket. They always hung over the side like they could make a wild bid for freedom.

All that aside, he was still handsome—there was no question about that. With his wheat gold hair, tanned skin, and hard Nordic profile... Yeah, he was hot. Even sitting on the couch watching ESPN—in those same rebellious boxer briefs—his face buried in a popcorn bowl like a truffling pig.

Which pissed her off even more. They hadn't had sex in a century. Gwen almost wished that she could accuse him of adultery because then she'd have a reason to find comfort somewhere. Pleasure in something besides toys that needed batteries or a package of cookie dough.

Gwen wondered how hard she'd have to slap the back of his head to get some of the kernels to fly out of his nose. Every crunch was a million needles jack-hammering into her spine.

"Can you *please* chew with your mouth closed?" she growled from the corner chaise where she was trying to read. Actually, she was pretending to read and trying to remember the last time she was actually happy. It pissed her off even more to know her archenemy had been right.

Morgan told her if she made a man betray his vows, sacrifice duty and honor for her, that she'd be miserable. But what did she know? She'd seduced a man on the word of a lake witch and still didn't have a man of her own.

"Can you please *talk* with your mouth closed?" he retorted without even looking in her direction.

Of course, having a man wasn't all it was cracked up to be, as evidenced by the behavior of the current specimen. "No wonder modern women are screwed. Look at you. Lancelot du Lac, epitome of knight in shining armor and what kind words does he have for his lady fair? Talk of courtly love and flowery odes to her beauty? No. It's 'talk with your mouth closed'," she sneered. "You're no knight in shining armor, but a douchebag in tin foil."

"Well, if you were a lady fair, rather than a shrewish harpy..." He shrugged, still watching the game and unaffected by her tirade.

"I never should have left Arthur." She regretted the words as soon as they were out of her mouth. Gwen may have thought them a million times, but she'd never said them.

He stopped eating and turned to look at her for a long moment. "No." Lance seemed to consider her for a moment and seeming to find her lacking, added, "You shouldn't have."

His words cut deeper than any knife. Lance had wished away all of their centuries together. No matter that she'd just been doing the same thing. It was different to hear it from him. He was supposed bear the brunt of any of her emotions and still love her afterwards. She realized it was a double standard, but he was a man. He wasn't supposed to have hurt feelings, and if he did, he sure as hell wasn't supposed to react to them unless he wanted to lay siege to a castle with his bare hands or something else heroic.

She had loved him, once. And Gwen thought he'd loved her. He wasn't supposed to say those things. In fact as the years had passed, Lance was nothing like he was supposed to be, but Gwen wasn't what she was supposed to be either. So much for being virtuous and honest and good. She'd failed Arthur, failed Camelot.

And she wondered for the first time if all of those misogynistic scholars were right—if she'd broken him. If the fall of Camelot really was her fault? She'd always maintained they'd all made their own choices, but now she wasn't so sure. It was easier to blame him.

"How did we get here?" Gwen asked with a sigh.

"I don't know." Lance turned off the game and looked at her. "But I don't want to be here anymore, Gwen. Eternity is too long to be miserable."

"What are we going to do about it?" She cringed as soon as the words were out of her mouth. Why had she asked the question? Guinevere already knew what the answer was, but she didn't really want it. Even though moments ago she'd been plotting his demise, imagining a life without him was terrifying.

"Honestly, Gwen? I haven't been able to stand myself since we came to Avalon. We betrayed Arthur. We betrayed ourselves. In all the years that we've been here, never once have we asked his forgiveness."

"He never asked my forgiveness for trying to burn me at the stake either. I figured we were sort of even. And you know what? I didn't betray myself. Maybe you did because you were his friend. I was never that. I was chattel bought from my father to save a kingdom. I didn't choose Arthur as my husband. I didn't love him. So why should I live my life in a loveless, sexless marriage for some lines other men drew in the sand?"

"Neither of us should be in a loveless, sexless marriage." He looked at her pointedly.

"That's why you didn't marry Elai—oh." Gwen said as the impact of his words hit her. "You mean *our* marriage? I wasn't trying to throw the dish out with the casserole. I thought maybe we could try some role-playing, warming lube, and counseling."

"That's just it, babe. It's not going to work because I don't want it to. I'm done. I told you I can't stand myself.

But I can't stand you either. The sound of your voice hits a place in my spine that makes me want to gouge out my eardrums with a melon baller. There's no getting past that or working through it."

His words were a sword in her gut. They were horrible, and hateful. Not things you would ever say to someone you loved.

"Come on, Gwen. Don't act like you don't feel the same. Let's be honest. I could feel that glare you were giving me earlier. If you could have made my head explode, you would have. This just isn't sitting well with your queenly sensibilities since I'm the one saying it first."

She looked at him. Really looked at him. Gwen remembered what his mouth felt like on hers that first time. She'd thought the heat would incinerate them both, her blood turned to lava in her veins and it had been pure bliss. The first time he'd come to her bed—she sighed. Gwen thought she'd die without him and she wanted to be with him forever.

Forever was a long damn time.

"You can have the house, the gold—"

"I don't want any of that, Lance!" she cried. "I want you." Gwen swallowed the lump in her throat. "I want *us*. The way we used to be."

"Not even Avalon with all its magick is capable of giving you that."

Each and every word out of his mouth was another piece of her life crumbling away. After everything this was what it had come to? No, she knew this couldn't be it.

Gwen went to him and slid into his lap.

"Gwen—" He sounded embarrassed for her. She'd be double damned if she'd be ashamed of trying to save their marriage.

She kissed him.

The supernova of a thousand stars that exploded inside of her when he used to kiss her didn't even flicker. His hands sliding up her spine felt good, but not because it was Lance, only because she hadn't been touched in so long.

"It's gone," Gwen whispered, something inside of her broken.

He set her away from him gently, and it was bitter-sweet. It was the kindest he'd been to her in years. "I'll call you about getting my things."

With that, Lancelot du Lac broke his oath again, and left the lady fair.

CHAPTER

# THREE

MORGAN

"What you're saying is that you're plotting against my son and you want me to help you?" Morgan arched a brow at the screen. As soon as she'd seen the email from Aphrodite, Morgan decided a Skype session was in order.

"More or less." The blond nodded, a hopeful look on her face.

"Are you sure you want to match him up with a virgin hunt goddess? Don't get me wrong, I love Mordred. But the only woman he treats with any respect is me and that's because I'll blast him with a supernatural pox if he doesn't."

"No, no. He's perfect. You haven't been to Olympus for awhile. There is no one here who isn't afraid of Artemis. She seems to have forgotten the part of her history where she turned several men into *women* for pursuing her too ardently. No god is going to take that gamble."

15

"No *god* will, but my son should?"

"If she changes him into a girl, I can always change him back. Love and anything to do with it is ultimately in my purview. He'll be fine. I promise," Aphrodite reassured her.

"I don't know. It might do him some good to see what it's like in someone else's shoes. His last relationship was with Medusa *and* Circe. Together. Can you imagine the man hate on that island now?"

Aphrodite pursed her lips. "Okay, next on my to-do list... I think they deserve each other anyway."

Morgan laughed. "Artemis can stay with me. I'll throw them together at every opportunity. But fair warning, Mordred will be fine on his own. He's immune to your arrows, zaps, or anything else you throw at him."

"Damn it. I told Artie she could have anyone she wanted."

"And she can. He'll be curious why she's so confident. Like Dumbo and his magic feather. It'll all work out."

"I thought that was my line?"

"You could come, too. Aeron would be a nice break from Ares, don't you think?"

"No. He's Artemis's backup plan if Mordred isn't viable."

"What a tangled web you weave, my dear."

"Now I just have to hope I haven't wound it around my own ankles." Aphrodite laughed, but the sound was hollow.

Morgan pursed her lips and thought very carefully about what she wanted to say next. Aphrodite was her friend, and she loved her, but sometimes the goddess could be a little blind when it came to matters of her own heart. "Can I give you some advice?"

Aphrodite narrowed her eyes. "Must you?"

"I must. We've known each other a long time."

She giggled. "Since you made that love potion for Lance and Elaine."

That was going to haunt her for the rest of her rather long existence. "And I'm *still* sorry. Heartily and forever sorry. Which is why I have to tell you—"

"Oh Zeus, here we go—"

Morgan didn't let her get anything else out. "Ares is just not that in to you."

"What?" The Skype connection blurred out for a moment as the goddess's rage almost knocked the satellite out of orbit.

"*He's Not That Into You*. Read it. Know it. Love it. If he really wanted to be with you, Aphrodite, he would."

"It's not in his nature. He likes conflict. He's the God of War for fuck's sake."

Morgan sighed. "I'm telling you, read the book. Stop rationalizing his behavior. You're a goddess, the Goddess of Love and you should be treated better. Right now, you're a booty call. He acts up to make you come to him so you think it's your idea. Then he doesn't have to commit or offer you anything but his war hammer. I know it hurts and it sucks, but just think about it, okay?"

"After I've thought about it, then what? Maybe Ares is just a booty call to me, too. I'm the Goddess of Love. I know what's in Ares' heart."

Morgan knew that Aphrodite didn't want to lose face. She could understand that. Love was often accused of horrible things. Morgan definitely sympathized with that. "If it makes you feel better to think so. But you know, Arthur is still single. You could do worse."

"Oh, heads up on that—I don't know how long that will be the case. Guinevere is about to be a free woman."

Something warm flared inside Morgan. Something she didn't want to acknowledge. "She's leaving Lance?"

"No, Lance is leaving her. He hasn't loved her for a long time." Aphrodite smiled. "You can be his cleavage to cry on."

Morgan refused to think about that. Lance hated her for what she'd done and the last cleavage he had any interest in was hers. Even though she wished it could be different. The raven at the door squawked indicating Morgan had a customer. "Duty calls. I have to go." She closed her laptop without waiting for Aphrodite's reply and went to the shop's counter.

The Witch's Brew probably wasn't the best name to inspire confidence in her customers, but it made her laugh. It was also apt because her place of business was a restaurant, but there was a little bit of this, and a little bit of that in the gift shop too. Morgan continued to take commissions for potions, charms and curses.

So when she emerged from the back of the shop, she was surprised to see *him* standing there.

Lancelot.

Looking every bit as perfect as the day he'd come to Camelot. Only instead of shining armor, he was wearing jeans and a t-shirt, but damn if they didn't look even better on him than the armor.

Jackass. He shouldn't be allowed to walk around looking so perfect when she couldn't have him.

"Hey, Lance." He still made her breathless, which was completely stupid because he'd never in a *million* years want anything to do with her. She was an Evil Enchantress, after all.

"Got any Johnny Walker Black?"

"Glass or bottle?" She could tell by the drawn and haggard look on his face he'd had a rough time.

"Bottle. Unopened."

"Sure." She tried not to be hurt he still wouldn't take anything that she'd opened. Not that she blamed him. She'd given that potion to Elaine that made him think she was Guinevere. If Morgan could take it back, she would have.

Morgan passed the bottle to him. "You okay?"

"I don't really want to talk, witch. I just want to go for a swim in my Walker." He pushed some gold at her across the counter and his long, strong fingers closed around the bottle.

She tried not to watch him as he sat down in a corner booth, but she couldn't help it. He was like the sun, so bright it hurt to look at him. Even while he tried to drown his sorrows.

Aphrodite had been right. Morgan would like nothing better than to be his cleavage to cry on. In fact, it would be better for all concerned if he just drowned his sorrows in her rather than that bottle of Johnny.

Before she could think better of it, Morgan sliced him a piece of cherry pie and took it over to his table.

This had bad idea written all over it, but Morgan had never worried too much about being good.

"There's nothing pie can't fix." She smiled. "Or at least *my* pie." While Morgan meant that exactly as it sounded, Lance didn't catch the subtlety.

Or if he did, he obviously thought she meant it was bespelled.

"It's not going to bite you back." She swiped her finger down the side of the pie, coating it in the sweet cherry filling and popped it into her mouth. "See?"

His gaze focused squarely on her mouth, and Morgan decided to live up to her wicked witch enchantress reputation. She couldn't have resisted even if she'd tried. Her tongue darted out to get the last bit of cherry and she swirled her tongue over her fingertip. "Damn, I have good pie. I think I'll have a piece."

"Morgan."

"Yes, Lance?"

"Good pie," he mumbled.

And he hadn't even tasted it yet.

# FOUR

## APHRODITE

*He's just not that into you?*

Morgan had to be confusing the sage and cannabis again because there was no way Ares *wasn't* into her. In fact, after all the times he'd actually been into her, literally...

Love and War were opposite sides of the same coin. They just belonged together. Didn't they? Sure, they fought, but it was foreplay. There was a reason people said all is fair in love and war.

The fact that she was even questioning herself was ridiculous. She was the Goddess of Love. Her own love life should be an easy enough thing to sort out.

What did she really want from Ares? Weren't things fine the way they were?

She popped a chocolate covered coffee bean in her mouth and took another sip of Rosa Regale. Aphrodite savored the sparkling red wine—the stuff was better than Ambrosia.

Things were fine.

Except they weren't.

Aphrodite popped a whole handful of the chocolate covered beans into her mouth and crunched angrily.

"Morgan, you wretched witch," she grumbled, still chomping.

Okay, so maybe she was tired of everything being fair in love and war, because it wasn't. Ares never played fair. Everything was strategy and winning to him. He couldn't stand to lose. Not even to make her happy.

The last time she'd tried to push him on that they'd ended up with The Trojan War. She'd held her ground, but it had been ugly.

Her cell rang and it was him. As the mortals said, speak of the Devil... and yeah, he totally earned the capital "D." She decided to ignore him. Aphrodite was feeling raw and unsure of herself, which was itchier than a yeast infection and just as awful for the normally confident goddess—and not so fresh to boot.

When the air around her began to shimmer and her Rosa Regale went flat, she knew Ares hadn't taken the hint.

"Look what you did to my Rosa!" she admonished as soon as he was solid.

*Mmm. Solid.* His chest, his biceps... No, no. She had to focus.

"I'll tell you what I'd like to do to your Rosa, if that's what we're calling it these days." He arched one black brow in a rakish manner. "There's a story for the bards. Rosa and the War Hammer."

"You and Thor and your mighty hammers." Aphrodite made finger quotes in the air as she rolled her eyes.

"What do you know of Thor's hammer?" His dark eyes narrowed.

"How soon we forget. Remember that little wager we had about the American colonies?"

"No." His mouth tightened in a petulant expression.

"Yes, you do. The one you lost," she paused for effect, "because you're a *loser*?" Aphrodite smirked. Morgan was wrong; Aphrodite was at her most joyful when she was baiting him.

*He's just not that into me. Whatever.*

"You must be confused, sweetness. I never lose."

She snorted. "Oh, so... what you're saying is that you planned to make it look it like you lost because you *wanted* to make out with Thor for my viewing pleasure?"

"Damn it. You know how that was supposed to go. If you lost, *when* you lost, I was supposed to get a show with you and the goddess of my choice."

"So you admit I won?"

"That was in 1783 and you're still talking about it. Can we let it die?"

"No." As if.

"Fine. You won. But let's not forget the Trojan War, little Miss Love Conquers All."

"That's a concept that you should be comfortable with. They say war is hell. But they say the same about love."

"Who the hell is they?"

She groaned. "Are you going to get me another bottle of Rosa? All your angry vibes took the bubble right out of my bubbly."

"I like that it's red like blood, but the bubbles have to go."

"Says who?"

"Says me."

"And you're in charge of what, exactly?"

"You. And you like it."

He had a point. She loved it when he was commanding. At least in bed. By Zeus, that god had a tongue that could—

"Which brings me to my question. Why did you ignore my call? Just to be difficult and make me hunt you down? I've never met a female that liked to be chased as much as you do."

For some reason, that statement really pissed her off. She didn't know if it was because he was talking about chasing other women, or that he was so put upon that he had to take time out of his oh-so busy warmongering and hatebreeding to seek her out.

"No, actually. I didn't answer it because I didn't want to talk to you," she said primly, her polite demeanor masking her feelings.

The dark slashes of his brows crawled up into his hairline like recalcitrant, although well-groomed, caterpillars. "I don't think I heard you correctly."

"Let me help you with that. *I don't want to talk to you,*" she thundered this last in the Goddess of Doom voice that caused the Rosa bottle to shatter and what was left inside turned to vinegar as is spilled across the table.

A waste of some damn fine wine that broke her heart just a little bit.

"What's got your tampon in a twist? What did I do this time? Did I forget the millennia anniversary of the first time you farted in front of me or the first time you slept over at my temple?"

"Actually, you did. I've never slept over at your temple."

"Not for lack of invitation."

"Really? When have I been invited to stay?" She puffed out her chest and drew herself up, a scowl on her face to imitate his. "Thanks for the poon, Aphrodite. I've got to be up to cause unrest and mayhem in three hours. Lock the door on your way out."

He laughed. He actually laughed. "I've never said that."

"Look, I'm tired of being your booty call." He suddenly looked like a drowning man and the rope she'd tossed out to save him was a live snake. "I know love isn't your gig, so I don't expect you to say it all the time. Once would be nice."

"We've got a good thing the way it is."

"No, *we* don't. You do. And you know what? *I deserve better*."

"Who has been feeding you this crap? Why can't we just continue on as we have? We're happy."

"No. I keep saying it and you keep not listening. We need a break. Don't call me. Don't materialize without an invitation. In fact, why don't you find someone else to be your booty call?"

"You're just hormonal. Remember last time you got like this? The Trojan War. It ended badly. So we'll just forget—"

"Ares, I'm so tired of hearing about the Trojan war. It's over. The only Trojans I want to hear about are latex and they don't involve your hammer any longer. Morgan was right. I can do better than this."

"That's only because you lost." He crossed his arms and flashed her a smug grin.

"*Oh. My. Gods.* You're not listening to me. That's it. I've had enough." Aphrodite decided in that moment she was going to Avalon with Artemis.

# CHAPTER
# FIVE

## VIVIENNE

L ady of the Lake, Vivienne du Lac, decided as she crossed the meadows to Arthur's, that she had a guilty conscience.

She wanted to come clean—no, that was a lie. That little voice in her head wanted her to come clean, but Vivienne herself was content to keep her own counsel.

The pile of shit she found herself in started off no bigger than a faerie turd and somehow, it starting rolling down a great mountain of crap and now she was well and truly buried in it.

She'd never wanted this for her son, but half of his trouble was of his own making anyway. If he hadn't gone off half-cocked to ride to the maiden's rescue everything would be as she'd designed it.

Her plan had been ingenious.

Camelot had to fall. Nothing so glorious or golden could last forever. It had been meant to go down in history as a shining example for all of humanity to aspire. Equality. Justice. Love.

The love part had screwed it like a poxed whore.

And it was Vivienne's own fault.

Vivienne had tripped over her own stupid feet and fallen in love with Arthur. Engineering Gwen's downfall had been simple. She'd always reassured herself it had been necessary. The oracle had proclaimed it so. It also proclaimed that Morgan and Lance belonged together and their son would have become high king after Arthur.

But no.

Morgan had done her part seducing Arthur, even though it had dirtied her name in all the annals of history forever. They weren't even related. Morgan was the daughter of one of Avalon's priestesses and Vivienne had sent her to foster with Igraine. Vivienne could always depend on her to do what was expected. Even falling hard for Lance and then betraying him when it became necessary to break his attachment to Miss Purity with that potion for Elaine.

Morgan was worthy of all the bounty Avalon had to offer, unlike that wretched Guinevere. Vivienne had been angry enough to chew Excalibur in half when her son had come back to Avalon, dragging her with him.

But back to the problem at hand... everything was her own fault. Arthur never trusted another woman again and he'd been alone since Guinevere and Lance betrayed him. He was by no means celibate; part of the draw to vacation in Avalon was to experience the carnal talents of the great King Arthur. He lived as he always had—his home a golden castle on a hill surrounded by apple orchards set against an eternal blue sky. The main parts were open for tours and

Arthur frequently invited all manner of females to tour his private rooms.

She found herself singing, "The rain may never fall till after sundown—" But this wasn't Camelot. It was Avalon, and she was the freaking Lady of the Lake. It was time she started acting like it.

If she wanted Arthur, she should have had him. Simple enough. He banged everything else in a skirt, so why not her? Maybe that would get him out of her system. She'd been too caught up worrying what he'd think of her if he knew she was at the root of his every misery.

He didn't need to know.

She could still slap Lance in the back of the head. In fact, if he'd been within range, she'd have slapped him. Every once in awhile, she still sent him a psychic slobber-knocker. He had it coming.

Vivienne didn't see the attraction to Guinevere. So she was blond and petite. So what? She was self-centered, petulant, not very bright, and with no breasts or hips to speak of. Sure, she was the modern definition of beauty, but back when this had all gone down, most men wouldn't have looked twice at her except for the fact she held the key to Lyonesse and a ridiculously massive dowry.

"To what do I owe the honor of your dulcet tones?" Arthur said against her ear.

She shrieked and tripped, falling backward into the solid wall of him. He anchored her there, and damn if she didn't gasp like a maiden. Vivienne had to admit it was nice being trapped in his arms. He was so warm and smelled of sunshine, summer grasses and the apples of Avalon. She tried not to inhale too deeply. Vivienne could only imagine the horror of explaining to him why she, the Lady of the Lake, was sniffing him like a stray dog.

"Who said I was coming to visit you?"

"So you were just frolicking in my meadows?" He still hadn't let her go, his thumb tracing small whorls on her forearm.

"No," she fumbled. "Yes. So what? I'm the Lady of the Lake. I do as I please. Even frolic in my own meadows, as all of Avalon belongs to me."

"Do you do that often, milady?"

"What?"

"Frolic in your own meadows? You should get out more."

Vivienne didn't know she could still blush, but her face was suddenly hot and her body throbbed. She couldn't help but imagine his thumb in that same motion on other parts of her body. If she squirmed just the right way, his hand would be on her breast.

But she was above such subterfuge.

"Mind your tongue, lad. I'm not one of those goddesses here on a weekend to tour your castle or to check out your mighty sword."

"Ah, Vivienne. An array of witty ripostes spring forth both about my mighty sword and all the things I can do with my tongue. But a venerable lady such as yourself wouldn't wish to hear of such things." His devil fingers ghosted down her arm.

"History has shown that if you have to brag about either your sword or your tongue, both are most likely lacking." She was proud of herself for managing a reply.

"You know what I like about you, Vivienne?" His breath tickled her ear.

"I'm sure you'll tell me." She tried to sound unaffected, but feared she failed miserably.

"You tell it like it is. Your honesty is refreshing."

*Ouch!* "Your manwhore routine is not."

"Why, Vivienne, you're jealous."

"Not," was all she managed to squeak.

"Your heart flutters in your chest like a hundred butterflies." His hand traced from her shoulder to her collarbone and finally rested over her heart. So close to where she wanted him to touch her. Maybe she wasn't above subterfuge after all.

"And being the good friend and king that I am, it's my duty to help you."

Goddess, did he mean what she thought he meant? Her mouth went dry. *Oh yes, oh yes, oh yes.*

"I know just the god for you."

*Oh no.* "I think not."

"Why not, Viv?"

"Don't call me Viv." She spun around in his arms to face him, taking control of the situation. "You like honesty? I've got some more for you. I am jealous. Wretchedly. It burns with the fire of a thousand suns."

"I knew it." A smug smile curved his lips.

"But I don't want a god."

"Goddess then?" The smug grin melted into a perplexed expression.

"No."

She readied her nerve, chewed on the words before she was able to say them. Tasted them. Considered them wholly. This would change everything, but Vivienne had already lived with years of regret and guilt. So why not take something else she wanted if he wanted it too?

"Then what, Vivienne? What is it you want?"

"You."

"I always knew you had a soft spot for me." Only it wasn't Arthur's neck she'd wound her arms around.

SARANNA DEWYLDE

It was Mordred's. That little bastard. He'd used his magick to trick her. She shoved him away from her as he laughed.

Mortification and fury vied for dominance. If it had been possible in that moment for Vivienne to have an embolism, her brain would have popped like an overfed tick.

"What do you think you're doing?"

"It's not what I think I'm doing, but what I actually did. I tested a hypothesis. It seems I was correct and you harbor a certain *tendre* for our king. I wonder what he'll think of it?"

"You will not be the one to tell him," she growled.

"No, you will be. After you confess your sins."

One of Mordred's gifts was that he could see guilt. Vivienne had done a good job over the years justifying her actions to herself so she'd thought her secret was safe from him.

She drew herself up, cloaking herself in the mantle of her power. She'd ended people for less than what Mordred threatened.

"I gave you the gift of immunity to magick and I can take it away." She growled again, and realized she sounded like a dog—but that's exactly what she'd be if he dared meddle in her affairs—a rabid dog of war.

"Oh, come now, Vivienne." He yanked her back against him, obviously not intimidated in the least by her threats. "Yeah, come right now. It's been so long for you."

He was right. It had. Her body yearned for a connection, for touch. For something hot and intense.

Although, certainly not with Mordred.

"My father's not the only reason women come to Avalon, my Lady of the Lake."

She'd admit, as much as she was ashamed to, that for a moment she considered taking Mordred up on his offer. She had no doubt he was gifted. He was a bad boy, after all, one of the baddest of the bad. The bad ones were always brilliant in bed because they liked power and bringing someone else to the brink of pleasure and having it within their purview to hold them back or shove them over the edge was always a rush.

But this was the first sign of any interest from him ever. He was up to something. "Mordred, my love," she twined her arms around his neck again. "I don't know what game you're playing, but this fire is hotter than you can handle. You're going to get burned."

"I should enjoy that very much, Vivienne. After all, your fire is only one I *haven't* burned in." He looked pensive for a moment. "It's either you or Guinevere, but I don't think she'd pose much of a challenge. Do you?"

"Oh, so I'm a challenge?" She was still pissed off enough to smite him. How dare he? "I have a challenge for you."

"Isn't that what I just said?" He smirked, seemingly sure he had her. Simply because he was Mordred and women melted at his feet.

"By all the power of Avalon, I curse you."

"I'm immune." He smirked and tried to kiss her.

And damn if she still wasn't tempted. "To all magick but mine, Mordred." Power crackled around her fingertips.

His mouth was inches from hers.

"I curse you to fall in love with the next person you kiss."

That did the trick. He jerked away from her like her body was made of electric current.

"Why the hell would you do that?" he snarled.

"I don't know. The same reason you pretended to be

Arthur." Satisfaction bloomed. "Feels pretty shitty, doesn't it?"

He smiled again, cold and calculating. "That was why I wanted to play with you, Viv. You're the only one whose power matches my own. Although I wonder what it says about you that you think love is a curse."

"Don't you?"

"That's beside the point. You still have a whole dirty little basket of laundry to show to Arthur, whereas I've never kept my villainy a secret. Whatever shall you do?" He said this last in a faux dramatic sotto voice. "And all I have to deal with is love. Maybe you should've just cursed Arthur again instead of me."

He left her standing there in the tall grasses wondering what the hell had just happened while his long strides carried him toward the castle.

CHAPTER

# SIX

ARTEMIS

Avalon was not at all what she'd expected.

She'd assumed Avalon would be much like the Orkneys, especially with all the mist, but the place where she'd materialized was more like Bora Bora. The water so clear and blue, she could see brightly colored fish darting to and fro over a white sandy bottom. The sun hung high in a blue sky and the temperature was just right. Not too hot, but perfect for a bikini.

"This is just the resort. The other side of the island looks a bit more European as opposed to south sea," Aphrodite said.

"This is gorgeous. The perfect backdrop to lose the V-Card. I'm so glad you came with me."

"Oh! Don't let him talk you into anything on the beach. Even if you have a blanket down, you'll get sand in your bits. Unless you're on top, but it's your first time, so that's probably a no." Aphrodite wrinkled her nose.

Artemis was suddenly a little nervous. In theory, this

had seemed like a great plan, but now she was actually here. She was going to do this. She'd heard it hurt—of course nothing could hurt like childbirth. Artie helped deliver a million babies.

Of course, that was part of what had kept her chaste. Nothing was worth all that blood and pain. Nuh-uh. She was a goddess though, she didn't have to breed if she wasn't so inclined. If for some reason she was ever inclined to produce a squalling, pooping ball of divinity, maybe she'd get lucky and have inherited Zeus's reproductive skills and could make babies from her fingernails. That would be cool. No reason to send a wrecking ball through the party place to do that.

She scanned the horizon for her intended prey, but saw no one.

"It seems pretty deserted."

"We'll just..." Suddenly Aphrodite stopped cold and perked her ears. Not unlike a meerkat. Although, the look on her face was pure disgust, as if someone had offended her on an atomic level. Both as in the smallest bits of her being, and relating to the apocalyptic level of smiting that was about to go down.

"Someone on this island thinks much too highly of themselves."

"Uh oh. I'm never going to lose my V-Card. You're going to blow up the island."

"No, no. You just follow the dock up to the resort and ask for Morgan. I will be back soon."

"Don't blow up the island."

"No, I won't. But someone needs a lesson in both love and humility. I don't know who the offender was, but I'll find them."

"What did they do? Use love in a curse or something?"

"Yes!" The Goddess of Love turned a mottled shade that was not at all attractive. "Love is not a curse and I'm sick and tired of it being used as a weapon." Aphrodite disappeared.

Saying that the shit was going to hit the fan wasn't quite adequate to describe the terror Aphrodite would set upon the poor bastards.

Using love as a weapon or treating it as something dirty was the fastest way to flip her normally kind and fun-loving friend into a Bitch Goddess of Doom. Not that Artemis could blame her. It was a bad rap, but that didn't mean she wanted to be there when Avalon became a smoking pit boil in the armpit of the world.

After debating it for a minute, she decided to do as Aphrodite said and find Morgan. She couldn't wait to get into her new bikini and stretch out on that white sand. She wondered when she'd see Mordred.

She took her time meandering along the plank walkway that led to a large Victorian styled house that seemed completely out of place. A sign hung over the entrance that read *The Witch's Brew*.

Tiny bells jingled overhead when she opened the door. The inside was almost like a witchy Cracker Barrel, with one side leading to a shop and the other to a bar and grill.

She expected a beach theme, maybe some shells since the resort and cabins were next door, but as she was learning, nothing in Avalon was as she'd expected.

"Hey there," a slender, dark-haired woman called from behind the bar. Artemis was immediately jealous of her long, shiny black hair. Her eyes were supernaturally bright, like amethysts. She was definitely of fae descent.

"Morgan?"

"You must be Artemis!" Morgan's expression bloomed into a smile. "Glad you made it. Where's Aphrodite?"

"She had some business to attend to."

"Oh no. What happened? Don't tell me Ares pulled some last minute—"

"No, no. Someone used love as a curse and you know how she feels about that."

Morgan looked up at the ceiling and then peered around Artemis's shoulder to look outside. "Okay, Avalon is still here..."

Artemis laughed. "I know, right?"

"It is," a surly voice sounded from a corner booth.

"It is what, Lance?" Morgan sighed, an exasperated sound.

"A curse," he grumbled.

"Never mind him." Morgan waved off his comment.

"Yes, never mind me," he agreed, but the tone was pure sarcasm. "Another round, witch."

"Go home, Lance. You're drunk."

"Don't have a home. I left Gwen." With that, his head thunked down on the table into a plate full of chili cheese fries.

Morgan looked embarrassed. "Are you sure you want to lose your V-Card? Men are all horrible beasts."

Artemis laughed. "Well, my life coach says to get rid of anything I haven't used in the last year."

"You have a life coach?"

She grinned at the incredulity on the other woman's face. "No. But it seemed like a good thing to say."

"Can you excuse me for a second? I can't leave the knight in shining armor face down in his chili cheese fries."

"I'll help." Artemis sighed.

"You're a doll," Morgan said. "Although, this does put a

crimp in our plans. I'd planned to put you in the spare bedroom. If Lance really doesn't have anywhere to stay..." Morgan trailed off, but then a grin brightened her face. "This is perfect. You can stay in Mordred's beach house and we'll set Aphrodite up at the resort." Morgan winked at her.

Her common sense siren blared like a tornado warning. "Won't he notice I've taken up residence?"

"He'll give up his bed for a lady in need, my dear. He may be a bad apple, but he's polite about it."

Morgan plotted so easily against her own son and Aphrodite had said that she was the real deal, one-hundred percent wicked witch. She had to wonder just how bad boy Mordred really was growing up with a woman like her.

She shivered. Morgan couldn't be that bad. After all, she was helping a guy who'd passed out in his food and giving him a place to sleep.

"Well, that's always important." Artemis wasn't quite sure what else to say.

"I've always thought so." Morgan smiled again. "You're going to give him a run for his money. I can tell. Even though you chose him, don't show interest too quickly. Make him chase you."

"Like a wolf would run down a deer?" She wrinkled her nose. Artemis was the huntress, not the hunted. She wasn't sure how she felt about being prey.

"Yes, just like that. Let's get Sir Drinks-A-Lot to bed."

"I've got this." Artemis, being Goddess of the Hunt, was athletic. Or as some mortals would say, strong as an ox. She hauled the mountain of a drunk man over her shoulder in a fireman's carry and waited for Morgan to direct traffic.

Morgan pointed and Artemis carried the rather large package of man to an upstairs room and deposited him on the bed. He'd be handsome without all the chili and cheese on his face.

Or the liquor on his breath.

"He's kind of pretty."

"He's a lot pretty. He's Lancelot. It comes with the territory."

Was that a sigh she heard on the lips of the great Morgan Le Fey? "I see."

Morgan flashed a guilty expression. "It sucks. He hates me and he'd probably rather sleep on the street than under my roof." She shrugged.

"Aphrodite would zap him if you wanted her to," Artemis said, thoughtful.

"I know. But I already did him dirty once. I wouldn't do it again."

"He'd never know."

"*I'd* know."

Interesting. Avalon continued to surprise her. Morgan wasn't evil incarnate as the stories had led her to believe.

"Listen, before you get the wrong idea—"

"Oh, hey." Artemis held up her hands. "My lips are sealed. Your soft and chewy center, at least where this guy is concerned, is still secret."

Morgan eyed her carefully. "I'm going to trust you. Don't dick me down."

"Wouldn't dream of it." No, Artemis definitely didn't want to be on the wrong side of the legendary Morgan Le Fey.

"Good. Because I'm your future mother-in-law. Wouldn't want to start out on the wrong foot."

"Not at all." And in the name of not starting out on the wrong foot, Artemis decided *not* to correct her assumption. She'd wondered why the other women would be so quick to set up a one night stand for her son. If she'd been mortal and used to mortal morality, it might have squicked her out just a tiny bit.

But no. The conniving woman was plotting for evil-imp grandbabies. That motivation she'd seen a million times before, and since becoming goddessmother and aunt to little Ephie, she could understand it.

Morgan led her through the rest of the upstairs living area and then out a backdoor onto a deck where she could see Mordred's "beach house."

It was a sleek, ultra modern monster, with walls of windows, a swimming pool on the roof, and a private beach.

"I'm never leaving," she murmured.

"There's an apple tree on the other side of the house, but it's enchanted. If you're missing home and want figs or pomegranates, it'll be happy to supply you. All you have to do is ask. Same with the house. If you can't find something, ask and it shall appear. After all, it's not a vacation if you can't find the toilet paper, right?"

Artemis laughed. She found herself liking Morgan more and more. "Yeah, that would be awkward."

"The door's unlocked. I have to get back inside to my customers."

To Lance was what she meant, but Artemis kept that to herself. She thanked Morgan and followed the small path to the house.

The inside was just as magnificent. It was a large, open floor plan with lots of white marble and large, overstuffed furniture. What she liked especially was that the inside of the house smelled of the sea and lemons. It was crisp and fresh.

She wandered into the single bedroom and the whole

far wall was a window that looked out across the azure water. What a view. Artemis sighed aloud. Even without the whole seduction angle, this was going to be a nice vacation. She hadn't had one in a century.

Artemis peered into the bathroom and almost had a showergasm. Not to be confused with self-love from the shower nozzle, but an actual showergasm. The white marble theme continued into what could only be called a wet room. Continuous waterfalls poured from the ceiling on three sides and soft lights twinkled around the space.

Dear gods! She wasted no time stripping and immersing herself in the decadent shower. She moaned aloud when the hot water tumbled over her.

Invisible hands startled her when they soaped up her hair, but the feeling of firm fingers massaging her scalp quickly squelched any reservations. Tension slipped away with the water that sluiced down her body. Why didn't Olympus have these enchantments?

Artemis moaned again. She couldn't help it. Nothing had ever felt so decadent.

"I can honestly say that this is a first for me." A velvet baritone voice startled her, but she didn't make any move to cover herself. She might be a virgin, but she wasn't body shy.

She pushed her wet hair out of her face and opened her eyes to see a man that could only be Mordred Le Fey. He had the same dark amethyst eyes as his mother. Fucking Tartarus, no man should have eyes like those. They made her wonder if she could be impregnated just from his regard.

By the gods, he was beautiful. His skin was like the white marble that surrounded them, perfect and hard. The lines of his muscles were so wondrously sculpted, she wondered if he was a Greek statue come to life. The black hair that hung down to his shoulders wasn't raven like his mother's, but more like a blackbird's—iridescent with hints of blue and green threaded through the black.

Her eyes were drawn down to his waist where only a towel hung secured with a loose knot.

Artemis tried not to lick her lips. Only the worry that she'd look like a slavering hound kept her tongue in her mouth.

"What's a first for you?" she asked. Artemis was proud of herself. Words accomplished.

"Finding a woman in my house making those sounds without me." His gaze centered in on her breasts and her nipples tightened, making something tug low in her belly.

He was definitely Mr. Right Now. She wanted to know exactly what kinds of sounds he could elicit from her.

"Your house? Oh, sorry. Morgan assured me the house was empty. I'll be done in a second." She tilted her head back under the stream for another rinse.

He laughed and Artemis was sure he violated some cosmic law. A man couldn't be that hot and have a laugh that did those kinds of things to her body. It was just wrong.

"Not shy, are you?"

"Should I be?"

"No, but this is another first. A naked woman who didn't come on to me."

He knew he was hot. Well, if the man had a mirror, of course he knew he was hot. Plus he was charismatic and a bad boy. They all knew their own appeal. She knew better than to show him he affected her at all.

"It seems I'm getting a lot of your firsts, which I would guess is highly unusual?" She twisted her hair to wring it out and tossed it over her other shoulder, exposing the huntress tattoo on her bicep.

Artemis rationalized it was only fair she would get to be first at something with him. It would be a fair trade.

"Highly. I'm Mordred."

"I gathered."

"Did you now?" His eyes roved over her and she returned the perusal and saw the thick, hard evidence of his interest outlined against his towel.

Artemis bit her lip so she wouldn't gasp aloud. Even as clichéd as it sounded in her head, she couldn't help but think she needed to pick someone else because that beast of a thing would never, *ever* fit.

It was just as she'd thought before; there was no need to send a wrecking ball through the party place.

"The eyes gave it away. I'm Artemis. And do you have a towel?"

"All I've got is this one, but you can have it." His fingers went to the knot at his hip.

"No, that's fine." She held out her hand and a towel appeared. "Seems the house found one for me."

"That was kind of it."

"Yes, it was." She wound it around herself.

"But such a shame."

He was such a charmer. She'd have her hands full, in more ways than one. "Mordred Le Fey, as handsome as you are, all the gilded tongue in the world won't work on me. I'm the eternal virgin, if you know your mythology."

"That's a theory I think we shall have to test, lovely Artemis." His voice held a promise that made her squirm.

"In your dreams, faerie boy. But thanks for letting me have the bedroom while I'm here." From the look on his face, it appeared both Aphrodite and Morgan were right. All she had to do was act unaffected. He obviously couldn't resist a challenge.

"You're welcome to stay as long as you like. You can even sleep in the bed. I'd never ask a lady to sleep on the floor." He grinned. "But seeing as it's *my* bed, I plan to be in it."

# CHAPTER
# SEVEN

GWEN

Gwen wandered around the house, unsure of what to do with herself. It was as if her life, even her skin, didn't belong to her.

She tried sitting on the chaise, but she kept seeing Lance sitting across from her, kept hearing him shatter their life together. It hadn't been a good life these last hundred years or so, but that didn't mean it wasn't worth saving.

The house was so empty. Even though Lance's things were still here, he'd taken something vital with him when he'd walked out the door. The quiet, rather than comforting her, was a heavy weight. She'd never felt so alone.

So utterly lost.

Not even when she'd first left Lyonesse to marry Arthur.

Part of her wanted to cry, but there were no tears. There was nothing but the emptiness. Loneliness. A dark, gaping hole that nothing could fill.

Except chocolate.

What Gwen really wanted was someone to give her the orgasm of her life, feed her chocolate, and hold her all night. That wasn't too much to ask, was it? And she wanted it to be Lancelot, but like she told him, not the man he'd become. The man he used to be. The gallant knight in his shining armor.

The man who'd loved her.

This Lance, she didn't know him very well, but what she did know, she didn't like.

Gwen had to face facts. The man she'd loved was gone. More importantly, the man who loved *her* was gone. What they'd had together had been dead for a long time. Lance moving out was simply burying the corpse.

If that realization didn't deserve a trough of Belgian chocolate gelato, she didn't know what did.

The little market at the end of Roundtable Lane delivered, but only on the off season. The owners had refused to pay Morgan to license a materialization spell and didn't have enough delivery faeries.

So it meant if she really wanted that gelato, Gwen would be hoofing it to the market. Maybe the fresh air would do her some good.

She shimmied into a pair of yoga pants, a t-shirt, and shoved her hair into a messy bun and jogged to the market. Not that five minutes of jogging would undo the damage she was about to inflict on her hind parts with the million calories of gelato, but it made her feel better about drowning her misery in chocolate.

That thought fell right out of her head like a brick when she arrived at the market and saw Arthur with a woman on each arm perusing the wine section. She could turn around and go home. She wouldn't have to acknowledge him; he wouldn't have to see her... Not that it was hard on him after all these years. She knew how he filled his time. He was a notorious manwhore. So notorious, in fact, he was half of Avalon's economy.

She knew she had no reason to feel jealous. She'd left him of her own free will, but that didn't mean she wanted to know he'd banged the backside out of half the supernatural population.

The question remained: Would she really let her ex and his double trouble flavor of the day keep her from her precious gelato? The answer was no. Hell, no. If she slunk away, it would be as good as admitting she was wrong, or regretted her decisions, or a whole host of other crap that she'd never cop to in a million years.

One thing she would admit—because there was no denying it—whoredom looked good on him. Just the thought... even her own phrasing pissed her off. She'd been painted with the whore brush for leaving him for one man and her name was a big smear of crap in the history books while Arthur was praised and admired for shagging anything that moved. It was completely unfair.

*Especially* since it looked so good on him. It had been a while since she'd seen him, maybe fifty years? A sad fact, that. They lived on a bloody island and she'd managed to avoid him for fifty years.

He laughed at something Bimbo Number One said and the faint lines around his eyes crinkled, giving him just a bit of an edgy appeal. He had streaks of gray at his temples, but it blended into the rest of his fawn colored hair. Although he was tanned, his skin didn't have that same sunshine hue that Lance's did—his was harder won. Lance's was genetics, Arthur's had been earned on the battlefield with long campaigns under the sun. Where Lance's fingers were elegant, a gift of his magical lineage,

SARANNA DEWYLDE

Arthur's were broad and rough. Even so, he still carried himself like a king.

Why hadn't she noticed how good forty looked on him when she'd been married to him? She shook her head, rattling those ideas out of her head. Gwen knew it was simply a case of "the grass is greener" because she was newly jilted and seeing him with other women had always irritated her. Nothing more serious than that. She wasn't actually jealous.

*Onward, little soldier, gelato relief is in sight.* Maybe she'd even ask if they had any of that wine ice cream and get some of that, too.

"What soft light through yonder window breaks? It is the east and Guinevere the sun," Arthur recited when he saw her, giving her a courtly bow.

Yeah, she was the sun all right. A bright shining light of humiliation in her too tight yoga pants that had never seen a yoga workout. She hated him a little bit in that moment because she knew he wasn't being ungallant. He always said kind things to her when he saw her.

Compliments she knew she didn't deserve. The sun, she thought again. Hardly. Why couldn't he be mean and spiteful? She'd deal with it better if he'd been outright cruel to her.

"Hello, Arthur. You're looking well."

Damn. Why had she said anything about how he looked? Now he'd feel honor bound to return the nicety and she knew she looked like refried hell. She made it a point not to look at Bimbo Number One or Bimbo Number Two. As far as she was concerned, they weren't there.

He gave her a lopsided grin. "Ladies, this is Guinevere."

Double damn. She smiled at them, even though it hurt

and she'd rather have knocked out her own teeth with a claw hammer.

"And Guinevere, these are... the ladies." From his phrasing, she knew he'd forgotten their names.

"*She's* the reason you're single?" Bimbo Number Two asked. "No, really. Her?"

"Forever and always." But his words seemed meant for Gwen alone.

She was imagining things. Had to be.

"Oh, Arthur. You could still turn any damsel's head," Gwen said, the sentiment bittersweet.

"Turn your head all you want, but he's busy tonight," Bimbo Number One supplied as they each tucked themselves against him.

Gwen wasn't about to get into some kind of contest with Arthur's *Slag du Jour*. So she simply smiled. "I can see that."

While Arthur had the look of a man supremely satisfied with himself, he said, "I'll be free tomorrow, Gwen. If you'd like to come to the castle for lunch and catch up. It's been what, fifty years?"

She swallowed. "Yeah. A long time."

"You can bring Lance, if he'd like to come."

Daggers shot through her heart and tore upwards, shredding the stupid thing. Of course he'd invite Lance. Arthur still cared for both of them. Even after what they'd done. Gwen felt lower than a dried out dragon turd.

"Tomorrow? No, you'll still be busy," Bimbo Number Two interjected.

"Ah, we shall see about that, my pet. We shall see." Gwen watched with horrible fascination as Arthur slid his hands over each woman's hip and guided them toward the checkout.

SARANNA DEWYLDE

She sagged and exhaled heavily. Would she go? Gwen looked up to study Arthur's retreating form, but he watched her over one of the bimbo's heads. "Noon?" he mouthed.

Gwen found herself smiling and she nodded.

Stupid head. She hadn't given it permission to nod. Gwen couldn't go to the castle. Panic set in. There was a reason she hadn't seen him for fifty years. They couldn't do this just friends thing.

No. No. No. And more no.

The place probably smelled like a cannery with all the pussy that had been in and out of there.

Gwen didn't really want to be seen making the trek to the castle either. Everyone on Roundtable Lane would be talking about it, especially since Lance had just moved out.

How did she get herself into these things?

She scanned the freezer case for the gelato and of the horrors that had been inflicted on her today, this one was the one that made her scream.

They were completely out of gelato.

# CHAPTER
# EIGHT

## MORGAN

She was determined not to be that creepy chick that perched over a man and watched him sleep.

But it took every ounce of her formidable will. Morgan rarely had such a chance to study him at her leisure, but she reminded herself if she woke up and found someone she'd declared untrustworthy staring at her while she slept, she'd smite them with the dirtiest, nastiest curse she could fathom.

Just to be on the safe side.

Of course, the same rules didn't apply because Morgan knew better than to trust anyone.

So instead of eye-humping Lance, she curled up on the sofa in the TV room to catch up on *Game of Thrones*. She'd started watching because the actor that played Jaime Lannister looked a little bit like Lance. The hair, for sure, the jaw if she squinted. She'd kept watching though because she couldn't stop. It was crack.

She loved that the good guys didn't always win.

Morgan had a whole season to watch, so she was sure that would keep her out of trouble. At least until Lance slept off his Johnny Walker induced coma and left.

She managed to get lost in the intrigue until Lance wandered out from the bedroom and peered into the TV room. He seemed a little lost, so she waved him inside.

"Come on in. I'm just catching up on some brain candy."

He sat down on the couch next to her, his weight depressing the overstuffed leather cushion. "I love this show."

"Watch it with me then, if you don't mind waiting for me to catch up."

"I've seen this episode, but that's as far as I've gotten."

She snapped her fingers and two tall, frosty glasses of rich, dark beer appeared along with an array of hot wings, loaded potato skins, and mozzarella sticks. He accepted the beer and a plate with a smile and they watched in silence.

Morgan couldn't pay attention to a damn thing that happened on the screen. She was sitting next to Lancelot du Lac watching television. It was as banal a thing as could happen and yet, every cell in her body was singing the Hallelujah Chorus in Latin. His leg brushed up against hers and the warmth of him though his jeans seared her.

The best part was, he didn't pull away, didn't seem to be afraid that he was going to get infected with witch cooties.

Of course, it was pure hell, too. Morgan spent years dreaming of what she would do if she ever got him alone.

Absolutely nothing was what she'd do. All she could do was sit there and cream in her knickers because the man's leg rubbed up against her. How pathetic was that? She swallowed and reached for her beer, her elbow brushed his arm and more frissions of awareness shot through her like little sparks.

*So pathetic.*

She dreaded the end of the episode. That would leave moments she'd have to fill with something.

He took the matter out of her hands when he spoke. "So did I really pass out in my chili cheese fries?"

"You did. After telling everyone who would listen that love was a curse."

"Well, that's humiliating." He pursed his lips.

"I run a bar, Lance. I've seen worse." She reached over and patted his hand. It was meant to be a comforting gesture, but it made her heart race.

"You've been very kind to me. You could have left me there, with chili and cheese up my nose."

"This is tourist season. Couldn't have anyone see the famous Lancelot piss drunk, could I? It would be bad for Avalon's image."

"Morgan," he began, his voice almost a whisper. "I don't know what your reasons are, only that you don't give a swish of tail about Avalon's image."

"I do so!" she cried. It was vital that he never know just what she felt for him. It would be too horrible.

"Well, thank you. Especially after I called you a witch."

"It was supposed to be an insult?" She smiled. "I am what I am. Witch. Evil Enchantress. Jezebel. Whatever." Morgan shrugged.

"You're no more a jezebel than Gwen. You haven't been with anyone in years."

*Gwen? Ugh.* She would ignore the reference and pretend the woman didn't exist. "How do you know?"

"You know how the Lane is about gossip. I would've heard something."

"You think so? Did you forget about the magick part? I could materialize in and out of Avalon at any time. I could have a nightly sexcapade tour around the world," she teased. It wouldn't do for him to think she was pining over someone. He wasn't stupid. He'd figure out it was him and then he'd look at her with pity and she'd have to kill him and then herself. It would be ugly.

"Trust me when I say that I could never forget about the magick part. But Morgan, I know you don't."

How did he know? "A lady doesn't kiss and tell."

"No. At least not until it suits her and she has a grown son to take over the kingdom." Lance closed his eyes. "Shit, I'm sorry. I'm just a dick. Ignore me."

His words found their mark, but she wasn't angry. Morgan knew what she'd done and she knew the price everyone had paid. "Lance," she put her hand on his again, this time curling her fingers around his. "I'm not Gwen. I'm not going to explode because you say the wrong thing to me. How can I be angry about the truth?"

"Just because it's true doesn't mean I have to shove it in your face. We've all made mistakes. I'm no saint. Look what I did to Arthur. It's wrong of me to judge you."

"Are you forgiving me for Elaine and the potion?" Hope welled inside of her.

"Yeah, I guess I am. If you want it." His face was so earnest, she almost felt guilty for her salacious thoughts. Almost.

"I want it." The words came out breathier than she'd intended, like the most wanton courtesan begging for her lover.

"It's yours." He squeezed her hand back.

Oh, why'd she done that? Grabbing his hand? She

should've just grabbed his dick and had done. She was so disappointed in herself.

Only, he didn't let go of her hand. He kept holding it and she wasn't inclined to pull her hand away.

"Morgan?" he asked halfway through the episode.

"Yeah?"

"Do you have any more of that pie? You make really good pie."

"You remember tasting my pie?" By the Goddess, it couldn't have sounded any dirtier if she'd tried.

"I do."

It was time to pull up her Big-Girl-Evil-Enchantress panties and go for it. If she didn't puke first. "What else do you remember? You were very drunk."

The tension in the room grew weighty with expectation and need. Morgan drowned in it, but it filled her up, fortified her at the same time.

He was silent for a long moment that seemed to stretch into eternity, yet she knew it had only been seconds when he spoke again. "Your mouth."

She leaned over him, her lips close to the waist of his jeans and her hair a dark sweeping curtain over his knees. "My mouth what?"

"Sucking the cherry filling off your finger." He was honest to a fault. How he'd ever lied to Arthur was beyond her. His every thought, his every need was inked across his face.

Morgan wet her lips. "Do you have pie on *your* finger, Lance?"

"I wish I did," he confessed.

"Do you really?" She brought their joint hands up to her mouth and suddenly, his forefinger was coated in the cherry goodness. Morgan licked one long motion up his

SARANNA DEWYLDE

finger before sucking it into her mouth and swirling her tongue across the tip.

"Christ, Morgan." His voice was hoarse.

With every swipe of her tongue, his cock jerked behind the fly of his jeans. She met his eyes and he tangled his other hand in her hair, his thumb stroked her cheek. He didn't try to push her down to his cock, but let her play as she would.

Morgan wanted this to last forever because she knew when it was over, things would change between them. He'd probably feel guilty because that's just how he was wired. She hoped they could enjoy each other, but she knew better. He was vulnerable and she was taking advantage of him.

Right after he'd forgiven her for the potion.

Ah, well. Such was life. She'd waited too long and he was a grown man. He'd lived a dozen lifetimes. He was experienced enough to say no if he didn't want her.

Yet, her twice damned conscience opened her mouth and operated it for her. The twat. "I'll be honest." *Why? No. Shut up. Just shut up!* "I want this, but I don't want any awkward platitudes or excuses in the morning." She punctuated the sentence by undoing the fly on his jeans, all the while looking into his eyes, waiting for him to tell her no. When he didn't stop her, she leaned in and tugged the zipper down with her teeth.

"Is this real?"

Morgan let go of the zipper and straightened. "Great. You're still drunk."

"Morgan, I'm not drunk." His fingers were still tangled in her hair and he drew her back over to him and she did a quick breath spell on them both since they'd been eating

58

hot wings. She didn't want her first taste of Lance's mouth to be hot sauce.

"Then what are you?" she whispered, bracing her hands on his biceps.

He closed the space between them, but he didn't kiss her. Instead he hauled her tight against him and dragged his stubbled cheek across hers, almost as if he were marking her.

His breath tickled her ear and one hand slid down her spine, while his cock pressed against the apex of her thighs. Just being like this with him was almost enough to make her legs shake and her toes curl.

"Living out a fantasy," he answered her. "Do you know why I really started calling you witch?"

"Tell me." She rolled her hips and worked her body against his.

"I thought you hexed me with a lust spell--" his lips were hot on the column of her throat "--after the Samhain Ball and that purple lace dress."

"That you spilled punch on."

"Because I couldn't stop staring at your breasts." His hand snaked around to cup her breast and she arched in to the caress. "You'd never worn anything like that before."

She tugged off his t-shirt. "That was the year I finally decided to stop hiding and being ashamed of who and what I am."

"What you are, Morgan, is beautiful. Why would you hide that?" He continued to nibble on her neck, sending jolts of pleasure ricocheting through her like bullets.

"I'm the Evil Enchantress, don't you know?"

"I do know." He thrust his hips upward showing her how enchanted he was, but then he pulled back to look at her face. "You can feel how much I want you."

She sensed there was something else he wanted to say. "But?"

"But I just left Gwen. I don't—"

Morgan put her finger against his lips. "No. None of that matters. No platitudes or excuses, remember? This is what it is. I'm not asking for love. I'm not asking for forever. Just right now." She leaned forward again, pressing her breasts against his chest. "Well, maybe tomorrow, too. As long as it takes to get you out of my system."

"Morgan," he began, still serious. "You'll probably be over it after tonight. It's not going to be anything to write home about. I don't even remember the last time with Gwen, it was that long ago." She laughed and he scowled at her. "I'm serious."

"You know, I've got a special kind of magick." For a second, he looked terrified, but his cock stayed rock hard. "Not that kind. Although, I could, but only if you wanted. No, lover, what I have is called Foreign Womb. Your dick will be like all the tourists that come to Avalon and want to see all the sights and ride all the rides." She grinned and then dragged her cheek against his in the same manner as he'd done to her. Morgan liked the way his scruff felt scratching over her.

"*All* the tourists?" he teased.

"Maybe. That's my business."

They laughed. "Laughing with someone feels almost as good as this." He grabbed her hips and pulled her forward to emphasize his point.

"Good. Then after you fuck me, we'll watch Robot Chicken, eat popcorn and drink beer in bed."

While Morgan meant it as a joke, Lance suddenly looked so hopeful it hurt. "Really?"

"Yeah, really. Now shut up and put out."

"Your wish is my command, witch."

This time, she didn't mind it so much when he called her witch and definitely didn't mind when he took charge, dragging her mouth down to his.

Their lips touched and Morgan was lost in him. If she'd thought she was drowning before, that had been like going under in a clear lake, this was being swept away in a tsunami.

Morgan was utterly consumed, from the taste of his mouth, his scent, the heat of him wrapped around her. This was everything she'd ever wanted.

And she realized she was a damned liar.

She loved Lancelot with every fiber of her being. Morgan didn't care if he fucked her until dawn, or was in and out like a Check N' Go. She just wanted to be with him.

Deep down, she'd always known her feelings were more than even what she admitted to herself. Denial had been a fine state because she'd never thought there was a chance in hell he'd touch her like this, want her.

Morgan knew better than to think this was anything more than rebound sex for Lance. She decided then that when this fling was done, whether it be ten minutes from now or ten days from now, she wouldn't grieve for what was past or what could never be. That's what magick was for—to wipe away the memories and pour cement into the cracks in her heart.

His touch, while passionate, was reverent. He didn't tear at her clothes, but removed them slowly, marveling at each bit of newly revealed flesh, touching her everywhere. He told her that her skin was like silk and moonlight.

Silk and moonlight. Who said those things?

Lancelot du Lac, disgraced Knight of the Round Table, that's who.

He pressed her down into the couch and she loved the feel of him, his body a solid weight. It reminded her this wasn't a fantasy.

Morgan had been wrong; she was the one who felt like a tourist. She wanted to see every attraction, commit each moment to memory so she could remember when she had to go home—the texture of his skin, the way the light played in his hair when he dipped his head and kissed down her body, and the searing pleasure that his every caress wrought in her.

"Now! Please, Lance!" she begged, needing him inside of her.

"When I imagined doing this to you," he began, kissing down her belly, over to her hip, and then the inside of her thigh. "You'd put a spell on me, forcing me to worship at your feet. You're wearing that purple dress, and worship I do. Starting with your pretty little ankle, I work my way up with my tongue, my lips, and my fingers until your sweetness is all over my face." His breath ghosted over her mound. "Now that I'm here, will you deny me the taste of you?"

"I'll never deny you anything," she confessed. Although she was afraid by the time he was done with her, she'd have burned so hot there'd be nothing left but ash. Visions of him living out his fantasy crashed over her. Did he wish to be commanded? The idea sent a stab of need ripping through her.

The first touch of his mouth to her cleft was lightning through her veins and made her cry out. She carded her fingers through his hair and arched up into the sweet torture of his tongue.

He laved and teased, pushing her ever higher until her body was strung tight as a bowstring, but he didn't stop, not until she was fisting his hair and dragging him away while tremors and aftershocks ricocheted through her.

Lance kissed his way back up to her mouth and while she tasted her own honey on his lips, he pushed inside of her. Morgan hooked her legs around his hips and arched up to meet every thrust.

"Morgan," he growled against her ear when she dug her fingernails into the hard, corded muscles of his back. "Now would be a good time."

"For what?" she gasped, still writhing under him.

"*That* magick. You're too hot, too tight." He punctuated each descriptor with another hard thrust. "Use me, witch. Use me until it hurts, until every nerve ending burns and there's nothing we've left undone."

His words caused her clench and he stilled, a ragged sound torn from him.

Did he know what he was asking her? All of those years being afraid of her magick and now he was asking to be enchanted, and using his cock no less? Lancelot was surrendering himself to her completely. *Use me.* By the Goddess, she'd hear that every time she touched herself from now until the end of time. He couldn't have said anything hotter if he'd tried.

Her magick flowed between them, hot and sweet. "Until it burns, Lance," she promised.

# CHAPTER
# NINE

APHRODITE

O f all the bloody nerve! Aphrodite knew who the culprit was; the fiend who'd used love as a curse.

Vivienne du Lac, Lady of the Lake.

This was the last straw. Yes, it was. The straw that broke the Cyclops' back. Vivienne meddled in the affairs of the love for the absolute last time. She had her athame so far up her own ass she actually thought she was in charge of something.

Aphrodite hated that about immortals who weren't gods. They had such a narrow view of eternity and their place in it. Aphrodite was ready to drop a bomb on her that would leave nothing but a mushroom cloud.

She materialized in the middle of a field, Arthur's castle in the distance. Aphrodite plucked through the threads of Fate to see just what Vivienne had screwed up before obliterating her.

Aphrodite quickly took in the scene that had knotted

the threads of Fate and used love as a curse. Vivienne standing there looking gobsmacked and a love-cursed Mordred walking away.

Hmm. The Mordred angle could be good for Artemis. Reformed bad boys made the best husbands and that was really what she'd wanted for her friend—a forever, enduring kind of love. Not just a quick punch to the V-Card. Of course if she'd outright told the other goddess that, Artemis never would have set foot on Avalon.

This could actually help her cause.

Vivienne still pissed her off, though. Love was not a thing to be trifled with or used as a curse and the Lady of the Lake had not yet learned that lesson. Something had to be done.

"Why are you spying on Vivienne?" A male voice, low and raspy like the sound of a blade on a whetstone startled her.

"Holy Zeus," she shrieked at the intruder. "Don't sneak up on a goddess like that."

When her heart settled back in her chest, she took a good look at the newcomer and decided that she liked what she saw. He was big, as most immortal god types happened to be, towering over her. He was dressed like a Roman Centurion who'd lost the top half of his costume.

He was deliciously, decadently, shirtless. A green tattoo of a griffin spanned from where its head was inked on his neck all the way down his torso where the animal's feet disappeared beneath the hammered metal of his belt. She could see the tail wound down around his thigh and disappeared in his leg guards. Green tattoos covered his arms from wrist to shoulder and Aphrodite couldn't make them out without closer inspection. Short-swords hung at his hips and she found her eye drawn to that line where his lower abs met his hips. The thing was like some swami, hypnotizing her.

"Sorry, I thought we were sneaking. You didn't exactly materialize where everyone could see, now did you?"

"What are you, Vivienne's keeper?"

"You could say that," he agreed congenially.

"Well then, you're in for a shitstorm, too." Aphrodite debated making them fall in love, but decided that would be a boon to the interfering hag. This guy was too hot for Vivienne.

"Oh really? What did she do?"

Hmm. He didn't rush to defend the lady. Interesting. "She used love as a curse."

"She does that all the time."

"I know. And I've had enough." Aphrodite couldn't keep the fire out of her eyes or from gathering in a ball around her fingertips.

"Did she curse you?"

"Me? Why does everyone think she's so powerful? She needs to be punished for her lack of humility and meddling in the affairs of gods. She was given one simple task of establishing Camelot and now she thinks the universe revolves around her."

He shrugged and Aphrodite was still mesmerized by the shifting tide of ink over his muscles. "She is pretty powerful."

Aphrodite clenched her fists and the flames grew bigger.

"What's it to you, anyway?"

"She's banging around like two virgins in the dark in *my* domain."

"Which is?"

"Why twenty questions? Are you writing a book?" Aphrodite demanded sourly.

"Humor me."

"Why should I?"

"I don't like to name drop." He shrugged as if it were all beyond his control.

She snorted. "If I smite Vivienne is that going to start a pantheonic war? She's not a goddess!" Aphrodite found herself bordering on hysterical. She didn't want to explain herself to anyone, including Tattooed McBangable.

"I'm not trying to bust your balls, gorgeous. See I've got this side gig. My name's Aeron. I'm the Welsh God of Slaughter and War, but on my off days, I'm the Guardian of Avalon. So, yeah. If the smiting is unwarranted, I'll have to do something."

Oh, it would figure. She knew he was hot, and he'd been an option for Artemis, but it irritated her that she was attracted to him. "Another war god? Zeus Harold! Like Ares and his mayhem haven't bred enough hate in the world."

"Gods and mortals go to war over love, too. The Trojan—"

She smote him. She didn't mean to, it just happened. Flames erupted from her fingertips and billowed out like a ball gown of doom to envelope him.

He wasn't fazed, in fact, he grinned. Which impressed the hell out of her. Even Ares flinched when she smote him. Her goddess bits were burning just as hot as her power. Not that she needed to lust after any more war gods. Ares was quite enough on his own.

"I, uh, sorry?" She bit her lip. "That war which shall never be mentioned again makes me uncontrollably angry."

"I can see that." He brushed off the last of the flames,

but grinned at her. "That's a right Irish temper you have there, sweetheart."

"I'm not Irish. I'm Greek. It's an Olympian temper."

"I think at this point in our relationship seeing as you smote me, you could at least tell me your name and why you're going to smite Vivienne."

"Tenacious, aren't you?" She sighed. "I suppose I do owe you. I really am sorry. At my age, I should be able to control my temper, but the reason I'm even visiting Avalon is that I only have one nerve left and *everyone* is chewing on it. Especially Ares. I need a recharge. I'm Aphrodite."

"Ah, now I understand. The War That Shall Not Be Named will never slip past these lips again." He made an "x" across his heart.

"You're awfully congenial for a god of war."

"I'm the God of War and Slaughter. They are mine, but they are not me."

"You should tell that to Ares." She rolled her eyes.

"I've tried, but he's a stubborn ass."

"Isn't he?" Aphrodite closed her eyes and took a couple of deep breaths. "Here's what—Vivienne has used love as a curse for the last time. It's my domain and I'm tired of it."

"I'll give you my blessing on one condition."

Her brow furrowed. A condition? She almost snarled, but waited to see what he had to say.

"Let her feel the flames of love that you burned me with, but not with someone unworthy of her."

Aphrodite narrowed her eyes. How *dare* he tell her what to do? As if he was in charge of something. Well, he actually kind of was and she didn't need an international incident with which her almighty father would have to deal. No, no one wanted that.

"My problem is that she's using love as a curse, which

I've stated a thousand times. It can be a weapon, but not a curse if you understand the difference."

"Of course. I'm skilled in all weaponry. Even love."

She shivered and Aphrodite hoped that she wouldn't have to use him as Artemis's backup plan. He might just be the perfect weapon against Ares. She could find out once and for all how he felt about her.

"Are you really? We'll have to see about that."

"One can only hope to be found worthy."

"You're a slick one, aren't you?" But she was used to Ares, so it was unlikely he'd be able to double-talk her.

"Some say."

"I have a proposition for you, depending on how well you like Ares."

"I don't. He's an arrogant tool." His lip curled in disdain.

"That's kind of perfect. Would you like to make him miserable?"

"Definitely. He owes me money."

"I'm going to be staying at the resort. Why don't you stop by later and I'll pitch my proposal over dinner?"

"I'll bring wine. Rosa Regale, right?"

"I—yes." If Ares had ever offered to bring the wine she would've turned to stone like one of Medusa's victims. If he'd offered to bring Rosa, well, she'd crumble like an old cracker. Color her surprised.

"Until then, milady."

He disappeared.

Aphrodite couldn't help but wonder if he'd wear actual clothes to dinner or that little gladiator outfit. She wasn't sure which she hoped for more.

Enough about the eye candy and personal plots. She had to deal with Vivienne, who incidentally, was still standing there watching the place where Mordred had been even after he vanished.

She took her time now, scanning the woman's aura and peered into her heart. The fool was in love with Arthur. Why hadn't she seen it before? That was going nowhere fast. Arthur would always and forever be in love with Guinevere. No matter what she did or how she hurt him, Gwen owned his heart.

Aphrodite felt guilty for hating her. Love had indeed been a curse for Vivienne and it was Aphrodite's own fault. She should've attended to the problem and dug it out at the root before it had a chance to wind itself around Vivienne's entire being like a poisonous vine.

*Damn.*

Who would make her happy? Who would treasure her heart more than his own? Aphrodite sent out tendrils of her power, searching the island for someone who worshipped Vivienne not as the Lady of the Lake, but as a flesh and blood woman.

And she found it in the strangest of places.

Hector de Maris. He'd been sent to foster in Avalon at the age of eight, at sixteen he'd been taken into House du Lac. There, Vivienne had become the epitome of feminine perfection for the young knight. He worshipped her with all the ideals of courtly love, but as a grown man, he loved her as a man loved a woman.

Vivienne still saw him as the child that fostered in her house.

He was perfect. Their match would right a wrong, and the road to achieving it for Vivienne would be plenty of punishment for her transgressions. All in all, a good day's work.

She'd start with a little nudge. One to Hector to go visit

and another to Vivienne so she'd notice that he was no longer that young knight, but a man whose sword belonged to the Round Table.

*Sword.* Aphrodite snickered and couldn't wait to tell Artemis about these new developments. Although, it would have to wait. She wanted to give her time to put their plan for Mordred in motion first.

Aphrodite could admit she wove a tangled web, but it was all for the greater good.

"Miss me, yet?" Ares materialized with his arms around her.

"What did I tell you about following me?" she sighed, exasperated.

"Woman, I've known you for a million years. At least. When you say don't follow, that means you want me to chase. So here I am."

"No, I *really* didn't want you to chase me."

"Why, are you here with someone?" His grip tightened possessively.

"Yes. Artemis." She shoved him off of her.

"You know that's not what I mean."

"If you must know," she said matter-of-factly, "I'm having dinner with Aeron tonight."

"Aeron?" Ares snorted the name like it was the most ridiculous thing he'd ever heard. "Honey, if you want to get away from me, he's not going to help you. He's a war god, too. You just can't help yourself. Why not save us both the trouble and just come spend the weekend at my temple. We'll get take-out, it will be a good time."

"No. No. And no. I'm on an island resort. Why would I want to go back to your boring old temple on Ambrosia Lane?"

"Because I'm there. Our bed is there."

"Our bed?" she parroted, the last syllable ending on an impossibly high note.

"You're the only one I shag in it, so I imagine that yes, it is *our* bed."

"What about Hyacinth?"

"Look, we've been over that. I thought I had permission."

"Do what you want means I'm tired of dealing with it because I know you're going to do it anyway. It's not actually permission."

"Then why do you say it?" he growled. "Look, I didn't come here to fight. Unless it means we'll end up naked. I just... you want something from me and I'm trying to give it to you."

"I already told you what I wanted, Ares. I want you to admit either that you love me or that you don't. No more pussy-footing around. And I do mean *pussy*. You're the God of War, for fuck's sake. You should be able to speak about what you feel like a grown man."

"The key words there are "man" and "pussy". Those feelings develop deep in a vagina, which I do not have."

"What?" *Did he really just say that?*

"Men aren't wired that way."

"You are the dumbest creature on two feet. I can't believe I let you put parts of your body inside of mine."

"I'm just being honest."

"That's it. You need to leave. We're still on a break."

"So, just to be clear, we're on a break, meaning you're not going to shag me, you may shag other people, but I'm supposed to sit at home and think about what I did wrong? This is another version of 'do what you want, but don't really.' Do I have that right?"

"Yes."

"If you weren't so good in bed, I wouldn't put up with this. Just so you know that."

"Ares!" She stomped her foot.

"Later, babe." And he disappeared.

Damn it, but that god drove her insane. Why did she put herself through this?

CHAPTER

# TEN

VIVIENNE

S omething was rotten in the state of Denmark.

And Avalon.

Vivienne couldn't put her finger on what it was exactly, but she didn't like it. Definitely a disturbance in the force. Something more sinister than Mordred's earlier antics.

It had started like a buzz at the base of her skull and pricked down her spine in a succession of bee stings. The sensation was decidedly uncomfortable. After scanning the island with her magick, she found nothing amiss and decided that perhaps she just needed to recharge in the warm, soothing waters of the lake where she drew her power.

After she made her way to the lake, she stripped off her robes and waded into the steaming waters until she was immersed to her neck. The buzzing and stinging stopped after she titled her head back and let the healing, restorative properties cleanse and renew her.

When she opened her eyes, she found herself staring at a very broad chest. The pecs were smattered with a sprinkling of golden hair that narrowed into the most delicious trail down the abs where it and the real estate available for her viewing pleasure disappeared.

"Milady," the owner of the pecs spoke.

She looked up at his face. Holy Goddess, it was Hector de Maris.

No. It couldn't be. Hector de Maris was still a boy, had barely earned his spurs. She'd fostered him in her own home before he'd been knighted. He was her son's friend.

Slowly, her brain made the connections.

Lancelot was a grown man. Had been for some time. She'd accepted that. By that reasoning, since Lance and Hector were the same age, Hector was a grown man, too.

Nope. The synapses still weren't firing correctly.

Hector de Maris was a kid and this man was built like... well... a man.

A big, strong man, she'd like to—NO. Not going there. This was Avalon, not Jerry Springer. Her brain was doing funny things to her because she'd gone so long without sex while pining over Arthur.

This wouldn't do. Not at all. She should've made use of her personal guard a long time ago. They were there to see to all of her needs, including physical. Only, it had been so long, she didn't remember who was on her personal guard. So many had gotten married and settled down once Avalon had retreated from the rest of the world.

Aeron had seen to Avalon's defense perhaps too well.

Then she realized Hector was still looking at her, expecting a response. They were both naked.

He must have seen her entering the lake.

Naked.

No, no. She wasn't naked. She was skyclad. There was a difference. This was ceremonial, her body was a vessel, she was working magick and—

And she had to stop lying to herself. Sex was a natural, normal body function. Vivienne wasn't wrong for craving sex; she was wrong for denying herself. Maybe that's where the buzzing in the back of her head had come from? She needed to refill the well in all ways.

"Lady Vivienne?" he asked, his big hand closing around her upper arm.

She'd been about to answer but his touch caused her magick to swell like dragon's fire and it erupted from her in blue flame.

Hector didn't hesitate. He swept her up against his hard chest and carried her toward the shore.

Vivienne found her voice. "I'm fine," she croaked.

He didn't stop.

"Hector." She used her best Hell-Hath-No-Fury-Like-the-Lady-of-the-Lake voice.

He stopped and looked down at her.

Vivienne was suddenly very aware of her bare breasts pressed against his chest, and of his brute strength, but most especially that he was hers to command. It was a heady rush.

"I'm in no danger. You can put me down." He could, but she didn't want him to. "It's just been a rough day."

"Then let me care for you until you are restored. You have long denied yourself the luxuries of your office and to do your duty to Avalon, you must do your duty to yourself."

"You're very wise for one so young, Sir de Maris."

"Youth? In the matter of centuries, what is fifteen years?" he referred to the years between them.

Nothing. It was nothing at all. Especially not when his

hands were on her skin. "I suppose those years don't seem like much after so long. But you will always be the solemn boy who told me he wanted to commit his life to the glory of Avalon."

"Vivienne," he began.

The way he said her given name was decadent. As if it tasted sweet on his tongue. She shivered.

"I have not been a boy for many years. I am a knight and a man. I have killed. I have bled. I have served Avalon. Served you."

This made her think of how she wanted him to serve her. Naked and on his knees...

"I meant no insult." No, she just wanted to control this reaction she had to him. Vivienne was in love with Arthur, so she shouldn't feel this for Hector. By the goddess, she shouldn't be in love with Arthur either.

For a brief moment, her twisted brain wondered if this was how Gwen felt torn between Arthur and Lance. Not that it mattered. She didn't need to see things from Gwen's perspective. More than that, she didn't want to.

Hector moved into deeper water, away from the shore.

"What are you doing?"

"You shivered and you are not yet restored."

Vivienne leaned her head against his well-sculpted shoulder. "Surely, you must have something better to do than haul me around the lake. I do have a personal guard, you know."

"That you utilize so rarely you've forgotten I'm on it."

*Oh Dear Goddess!*

"It is my duty and my pleasure to see to any of your needs."

She was sure her clit just exploded. Having him had just become a very real possibility. Any knight who accepted a position on her personal guard knew that seeing to her physical needs was part of the job.

That hand on her thigh could be between them bringing her to orgasm right here, right now, if she so desired it. All she had to do was tell him. Open her mouth and say, "Hector..." Yet, she couldn't even finish that sentence in her head where he couldn't hear her.

Even though she was Lady of the Lake, even though it was within her rights to use her personal guard in such a manner, she'd only ever done so once and that had been with Lance's father.

She preferred men to pursue her because then she knew they wanted her. With her guard, it was a duty. Vivienne wanted to inspire passion, lust, and need. She didn't want to be a chore or task to be completed.

"The lake is warmer here." He finally stopped after rounding a copse of rocks.

"I'd forgotten this was here!" Vivienne cried out in delight. He'd brought her to a small, yet exotic grotto where there was an abundance of plant life and thick, broad ferns spread their fronds like a curtain over the entryway.

"As I said, Vivienne, it has been too long since you've seen to your own needs. Or allowed anyone else to do so. Why do you deny yourself?"

*Because I don't deserve it.* That was a little more truth than what she was willing to share. But Hector was far more perceptive than she'd realized.

"Guilt is a heavy mantle especially when there is no reason for it." He eased her down onto a rock facing the shore and with gentle fingers, titled her head back into the water and massaged her scalp.

"You don't understand."

"Don't I? I was Lance's best friend. I know how he

suffered and I know what you did. If Lance and Arthur have forgiven you, don't you think it's time you forgive yourself?"

"No. Arthur can't truly forgive me because he doesn't know the depths of my betrayal," she whispered.

His fingers moved down her scalp to her spine, stopping just at the sacral dip, to work back up over her shoulders and down her arms.

"I'll be your confessor, Vivienne. I'll keep your sins."

She allowed herself to lean back against his broad chest while he massaged her, his hands moving over her body in the ritual she'd long denied herself. Vivienne knew she should tell him to stop because what she felt was anything but sacred and holy. It was hot and dark.

Her nipples were tight, stiff peaks barely concealed by the water. If she tilted her body just so, arched her back, he'd see and part of her wanted him to see her need, to fill her desire without her asking him or commanding him.

When his hands worked over her hips and thighs she couldn't suppress the moan of delight.

"You should stop," she managed. Vivienne ached. It was as if every sensor had focused on his touch and was drawing it down to her needy cleft.

"The veneration of flesh displeases you?"

"It isn't what it should be." Her voice was a hoarse whisper. Vivienne knew her confession was cryptic, but she couldn't bring herself to tell him his touch aroused her. The way he touched her was supposed to be adulation for the vessel—for her office. For her power. Not for her as a woman. Although, it was well within her rights and even expected of her to use her personal guard in such a way.

He stopped then, but didn't move away from her. "Have I offended you in some way? I only seek to serve."

"No, Hector." She swallowed. "It's nothing you've done.

You are all that a knight should be. All that the elite of Avalon should be."

Emotion welled sticky and vitriolic. She always said she refused to feel guilt, but that was a lie. A lie she told herself again and again until it had hardened around her like stone, but all it took was a little light to shine on her desires and it crumbled around her, leaving her bare and vulnerable.

Vivienne felt wholly unworthy.

Yet all of that slipped away when he touched her again. His breath was ragged against her ear; the solid wall of him behind her both comforted and aroused her. He kneaded the flesh of her thighs and worked his way to her belly, his broad and strong fingers so close to the center of her need, but so damn far away.

Hector tightened his grip on her, pressing her flush against him so she could feel his hard cock jutting up against her. "No, Vivienne. I'm not without sin. I covet. I *lust*."

He wanted her! This was everything she'd wanted; only it wasn't with the right man. It wasn't Arthur. Hector was handsome and strong, kind-hearted. But he was so young, he was Lance's friend, and she wasn't in love with him.

Even though she knew this would be the best sex of her life. He knew just how to touch her. Her body wanted him and her magick wanted him, even though her heart didn't.

"I'm in love with someone else," she blurted.

Hector pushed his fingers down her belly and between her thighs as if she hadn't even spoken. He slipped them inside her cleft teasing the engorged bud of her clit. "That's my penance for lust. Coming on my cock instead of his is yours."

His words made her blush. They were such a trespass,

SARANNA DEWYLDE

forbidden. Hector did indeed have a kind heart, but he had the mouth of a satyr.

Hector didn't wait for her permission or her protest, he hauled her up against him and she wrapped her legs around his waist. He supported all of her weight with his forearm and that in itself was a turn on. He could break her like an autumn twig, but instead he used his strength to bring her pleasure.

It was Vivienne who initiated their kiss, tentatively brushing her lips over his as he carried her to shore. Her magic flared, their energies twined and his strength infused her.

Vivienne's power soared, she'd never felt so alive, so potent. When using her personal guard, it was supposed to symbolize the joining of the god and goddess. She'd denied herself so long because the needs of her body weren't to increase her magick; they were for a more earthy satisfaction.

She was more than the Lady of the Lake. Vivienne was a flesh and blood woman with the same needs as all creatures.

Hector wanted her. She wanted him. There was no reason to deny them both.

He pushed her down in the wet sand, ripples of the warm water lapping at her feet as he kissed her, tasted the arch of her neck, the rosebud peak of her nipples.

When he buried himself inside of her and he brought her to the edge, one name was in her heart and a whispered benediction on her traitorous lips.

"Arthur," she cried out as Hector sent her spiraling over the edge of pleasure.

# CHAPTER
# ELEVEN

ARTEMIS

M ordred wasn't kidding when he said that he
meant to be in the bed.

He'd failed to mention that he slept naked.

Artemis did her level best to act unimpressed, but she'd
never actually been in such an intimate situation with a
man. She kept finding herself choking back this stupid little
titter that wasn't quite a giggle.

Which irritated her to no end. If she could've slapped
some sense into herself without looking like a complete
idiot, she would have. She wasn't some teenager looking to
score. She was a goddess grown who'd made a decision
about her body and her life.

So why couldn't she grab it—him—by the balls and just
say what she wanted? She could tell he liked what he saw
when she'd been naked in the shower. Why did they need
the hunt? It wasn't as if she wanted it to be a regular thing.

Of course, having that option might be a good thing,

she thought as she stole a glance at him only to find he was looking at her with those supernaturally gorgeous eyes.

"Straight to the pillow talk then? I do want to go to sleep sometime tonight."

"How would I prevent you from going to sleep?"

"You were looking at me. Have you ever tried to sleep with someone staring at you?"

"Mordred, you have to understand I'm going to be curious. I've never slept next to a man before. Of course I'm going to stare at you," she blurted.

"Now I'm curious." He propped himself up on his elbow. "How is it you can be eternal and not once have been overcome with passion? Or even loved someone enough to spend the night next to them?"

Artemis blushed, but quirked a brow. "Eternal? Are you making reference to my advanced age?" She'd never had anyone say anything of the sort to her before.

"Your age is a fact, my lovely. I didn't say you were a withered hag. I only said that you have existed for a long time without one of the best things our creators have given us."

Something about him made her want to be honest. That went against the plan Aphrodite and Morgan had laid out for her, but this was Artemis's experience. She'd have it on her terms.

Well, mostly honest. She wasn't quite ready to tell him that she wanted him to punch her V-card. Artemis was still a little afraid of the deed. Gods hadn't always been kind to females, be they mortal or immortal. It was why she'd asked her father to remain a virgin forever.

Though she was just beginning to realize that forever was a long time to spend alone.

She bit her lip.

"Oh, this is going to be good if it makes you blush and bite your lip." He flashed his white teeth at her in a smile.

"The last man who pursued me," she paused and took a deep breath, "I turned him into a woman. After that, no one was interested." She waited for him to push her out of the bed, or for him to de-materialize, or run screaming. Most men found what she'd done to be the ultimate trespass, even though her former swain would've forced himself on her if she hadn't taken drastic steps.

He didn't run, Artemis found that comforting, although his next question startled her.

"Is your interest in women, then?"

"That's kind of a personal question." And not one she expected.

"Sorry," he said, although he didn't look it in the least. "I've never had a conversation with a virgin before."

"So because I'm a virgin, you assume I'm a lesbian? Really?" She eyed him. "Wait, you've never had a conversation with a virgin? Ever?"

"Not to my knowledge. I don't generally speak to women I don't fuck. Except my mother."

"*That's* why I'm a virgin."

"Because *I* don't have conversations with women?"

"Not you in particular, but that mindset." She pulled the blanket up closer to her chin like it was some kind of shield.

"So you think everyone who has sex should be in love?"

"No. But they should respect each other."

"What does the banal minutiae of my day or yours have to do with how fast I can flick my tongue over your clit?"

Her eyes widened as she thought of him doing just that. "Nothing, but it implies you don't care about my day."

"That's not what I said."

"Isn't it?"

"Hmm. Interesting."

"What?"

"I think having my tongue in your bits is more intimate than idle chit chat about people who have nothing to do with us, but you think I should waste our time together talking about people and things that aren't relevant."

"They are relevant because they affect me. If we're in a relationship, even a casual one, you should care about what affects me." Zeus, how had this gone from a what-if conversation about two nameless, faceless people to being about them and what it would be like if they were together? She was in deep.

"That's probably why Circe and Medusa voted me off the island," he said, still no remorse evident in his voice.

"You were sleeping with both of them?"

"At the same time." He smirked.

"Hmm. Interesting," she tossed his words back at him.

"How so?"

"You can't maintain a relationship with one woman, so you try for two. Did you think that maybe they'd fulfill emotional needs for each other that you're not capable of filling?"

"Artemis, trust me when I say that I'm capable of filling anything that needs it."

"Another reason why I've chosen to remain chaste. We were having a serious discussion and as soon as I touched something you didn't want to deal with you had to turn it back around to your cock."

"I'm a man. Everything is about my cock. That's just how we're wired. Maybe you should go to spend some time with Medusa and Circe. In fact, I'd pay to see that."

"Who said we'd let you watch? You know, you're pretty, but you're a dick."

"I'm honest. And it's not always pretty. Truth is one of the sharpest blades in my arsenal, but the ugly truth is always better than a beautiful lie, don't you think? I mean, look at Camelot. It was a lovely dream, but built on the foundations of a lie that weakened it, couldn't hold it up when it was beset by evil and it crumbled to dust in the pages of history."

"That's what happened? I thought you and Gwen knocked it down."

"Oh, I was born to destroy Camelot. That was my purpose to exist, but I never would've been born if my father had been a righteous man."

"No one is perfect. Even the righteous fail," Artemis countered.

"They do. So what's the point of all that denial of self, trying to make yourself into something you're not only to stumble and fall on your face?"

"To be better than what you could've been."

"To what end?"

"I don't have an answer for that."

"If they'd indulged their desires honestly, with no judgment, do you think Camelot would've fallen?"

"Eventually. Nothing is meant to last forever. Not ideals. Not people. Not even gods." Not even her virginity.

"So don't you think it's time you tried something new?" His words echoed her thoughts.

"Oh, Mordred." She laughed. Artemis had almost fallen for it, but the huntress in her made her competitive. This was why she couldn't be honest. He played the game too well. He'd have had her twisted around his finger. She couldn't let him shift the balance of power or she'd be screwed. "You're good. All of this serious discussion. The intimacy of sharing our deepest thoughts. But if you think you're man enough to be first, it's going to take a lot more effort than that."

"I'd be disappointed if it didn't." He didn't look the least bit sheepish that he'd been caught. He even had the nerve to ask, "So, how about you just let me hold you tonight."

Artemis snorted so hard she almost choked on it. "That's the line you're going with? You do know that I'm the goddess of childbirth too, right? You know how many babies I've helped deliver who started out as a just-let-me-hold-you? Plus, you're naked under that blanket."

"That doesn't matter. I'm not going to do anything to you that you don't ask me to do."

She narrowed her eyes at him.

"I don't fancy becoming a woman." He winked at her, but when she scowled at him he spoke again. "I'm a libertine and a hedonist of the worst sort, but I like my partners willing."

"All you want to do is hold me?" Artemis looked at him, derision curling her lip.

"I didn't say that's all I wanted to do, but it's all I'm asking for. You're in my bed after all. The least you could do is keep me warm."

"That's what you're going to go with to get into my pants?" Considering his reputation as a master of his craft, Artemis found this attempt to woo her to be sadly lacking. There had to be another angle.

"Artemis, who said I was trying to get into your pants? You've been all of these firsts for me." He grinned. "I think I want to turn over a new leaf. We should be friends. I've never had a woman friend."

*Oh, you have to be shitting me.* She decided to turn the

game back on him. Maybe just a dash of that honesty she was flirting with. "So you don't want to be first? That's too bad. I guess I'll just have to ask your dad. He's the carnival ride all the women come to Avalon to see, right?"

He appraised her. "Looks like I'm a bad influence. Whatever makes you happy, princess."

"I'm not a princess. I'm a goddess."

"You may be a goddess, but you've been indulged like a princess." He smirked and then said in a falsetto voice, "Oh Daddy, I'm scared of the big, bad, men. I want to be a virgin forever." Mordred eyed her. "And Daddy indulged you, didn't he? You never had to learn about the world or the people in it. Never had to feel what humans feel, even though you have dominion over them. You get to sit in judgment, even though you've never felt what we feel."

*Ouch. That stung.* "I've decided I don't want to be your friend." She rolled over.

He laughed, the bastard. He was actually amused.

"I mean it. I don't like you."

"Good. Does that mean the pillow talk part is over and I can sleep without you staring at me?"

"You're not that interesting to look at anyway." Liar! He was so beautiful it hurt to look at him, and she didn't want to stop. Until his mouth started moving. "I like you better when you don't talk."

"See, now we're getting somewhere. That's how I feel about anyone I sleep with."

"You're insufferable." She'd changed her mind. No way was she giving it up to this overstuffed, pompous, pile of satyr crap. No way. No thank you. Artemis was going to call Aphrodite and see if she could set up a meeting with Aeron and in fact, first thing tomorrow, Artemis was going to get a room at the resort.

"Surely I'm not all bad. I can introduce you to Arthur, if you really want to ride the ride as you so eloquently put it."

"Shut up. Sleeping." Of course she was doing nothing of the sort. Artemis lay there, on that overstuffed pillow, in the lap of luxurious comfort as frothy as a rabid dog. She probably wouldn't sleep at all, but she be damned if she was going to get up and leave because he'd win.

"I'm just trying to be helpful, new friend."

"You're an asshole."

He laughed again. "Sweetheart, you haven't played this game. Did you really think you were going to beat me in the first round?"

"The same way you thought all that faux intimacy was going to work?"

"Hey, I was just trying to build a bridge. To friendship." His voice dripped with sarcasm.

"Fine. We're friends. Shut up. I'm tired."

"I win," he crowed.

"For now."

"For always."

"You're like a woman; the way you have to have the last word."

"Just putting my stamp of ownership on the conversation."

"If you don't shut up, I swear by Zeus I'm going to smite you."

"I'm immune to magick."

"Smiting isn't magick."

"No? Prove it. Smite me right here. Right now."

"Oh, you think I won't?" She flipped over and sat up.

"Yeah, smite me *hard*." The corner of his mouth curled up in a devastating smirk that made her want to kiss him.

So she did.

Artemis pounced on him like a great cat of prey and smashed her mouth into his before he could tell her no.

He kissed her back and she suddenly understood what all the fuss was about. Shooting stars, fireworks, symphonies... Yeah.

Only, he broke the kiss much too soon with a look of abject terror on his face. Instead of odes to her lips, or poetry about her sweet kisses, he said, "Son of a bitch."

# CHAPTER

# TWELVE

### GWEN

Gwen changed her mind no less than thirty-four times.

Both about going to Arthur's for lunch and what she would wear. She decided not to go four times because she had nothing *to* wear. Or nothing that looked good on her.

After comparing herself to Bimbo Number One and Bimbo Number Two, she couldn't even stand to look in the mirror.

It was just as well they were out of gelato at the market. Her ass couldn't take it.

Why couldn't the extra weight have gone to her breasts? They could use a little more heft and a little more lift. She sighed.

Really, she wasn't being overdramatic when she said that nothing in her closet would do. She had to be very careful about the image she presented or everyone on

SARANNA DEWYLDE

Roundtable Lane would be gossiping and speculating about poor little Gwen crawling back to Arthur.

That's not what this was. Not at all. She just needed a friend. Everyone on the Lane had always judged her, looked down their noses at her for her choices. Everyone but Arthur.

Lance never had to bear the brunt of what had happened. According to the gossips, he was an injured party just like Arthur and Gwen, well, she was the raging Whore of Babylon.

She and Morgan both.

But Morgan *was* a slut and a bitch. She hadn't been overcome with lust or love for Arthur, it had been for service to Avalon that she'd committed her sins. Cold. Calculating. The woman wouldn't know what love was if it bit her nose.

Not that any of that actually mattered after all this time.

She finally decided on a dress because she'd have to lie down to zip up her jeans and she didn't want to risk too-tight-jean-induced muffin top. Gwen already felt bad about herself, she didn't need to give that nasty little voice in her head any more material.

The dress she chose was a little rockabilly number, blue with white anchors and cherry bows on the poplin sleeves. It even had a crinoline, but Gwen didn't want to add to her posterior real estate.

Of course, she had no problem shimmying into the wonder bra that gave her some respectable cleavage.

Her now ex monster-in-law was always going on about how Gwen was too skinny, didn't have a good figure, wasn't fit for breeding. Like that's all she was good for was to be a brood mare. Instant baby factory, just add dick.

Gwen never understood that mentality. Lady of the Freaking Lake, a woman who commanded armies and she still wanted to shove Gwen in a mold and treat her like breeding stock.

She supposed that was why she drank the wild yam tea for the whole of both of her marriages. Gwen didn't want to get pregnant until she was ready and certainly not because Vivienne had told her to. She could take a flying fuck at a rolling donut. They all could.

With that in mind, she decided she didn't care who saw her on the way to visit Arthur. It was none of anyone's business what she did or who she did it with.

She finished getting ready and stepped out of her front door into the bright sunshine.

"Is it true?" Elaine stood on the steps, with her arm raised to knock.

And the hits just kept coming, Gwen thought to herself. Elaine was the biggest Lane gossip. She always had something to say about someone—probably because her own life was so lacking and miserable. Gwen used to feel sorry for her, until she got that potion from Morgan and pretended to be Gwen.

"Is what true? That Lance I have separated? Yes. He's all yours." She was like some kind of vulture there to pick at the carcass of her marriage.

"I knew that you separated. Is it true he moved in with Morgan?"

"I wouldn't know. I don't have time for this, I'm busy today."

"How can you not know? I mean—" She chattered on, but Gwen wasn't listening. Instead, she pushed past the annoying woman and began her walk to the castle.

Except Elaine chittered on behind her like a sparrow on meth.

"Elaine!" Gwen snapped when they got to the end of the block.

"Wow, you're so angry. First screaming in the market and now this. You should really do something about that temper. Is that why Lance left you?"

"At least I didn't have to pretend to be another woman to get him to sleep with me."

Elaine's mouth fell open and worked like a fish flopping on a dry dock.

"Nothing else to say? Good. Told you I was busy."

"Well, I never!"

"Obviously." Gwen left her standing there and marched with purpose to the end of Roundtable Lane where large meadows sprawled in front of her. She hadn't planned on traipsing through the grass in the shoes she'd chosen, so she took them off.

When her feet first touched the cool grass, she stood for a moment, curling her toes around it. This was the first time in years she'd gone barefoot in the grass. She took a deep breath, inhaling the menagerie of scents around her-- fresh air, green grass, and the apples of Avalon's orchards.

The sun warmed her skin and she found herself looking up at the blue sky as she walked. Clouds, white and puffy like big wads of cotton bounced around the endless blue. Not enough so that it was overcast, but just enough to make her think about lying down in the grass and watching them pass.

She and Lance used to do that, drinking summer wines and pointing out shapes or people in the clouds. They'd make up little stories about the characters they'd created and why it was either their reward or punishment to spend eternity as a cloud—like the Romans and Greeks and their stories of the constellations.

That used to be her favorite thing in the world to do—after making love with Lance. Gwen thought that she could spend forever doing those things with him. It was so strange to think that forever was over.

It didn't take her long to get to the castle. Her feet knew their own way. She'd lived there once. When Morgan and Vivienne had brought them all to Avalon, they'd brought much of Camelot too. Including the castle.

Every brick held some memory for her and reminded her of her betrayal.

Why had she come?

The question answered itself when Arthur opened the door for her before she knocked.

The first thing she noticed was the way his hair curled over the edge of his collar. The green dress shirt he wore brought out the subtle flecks of gold in his brown eyes. But what was the most devastating was his gentle smile.

He'd never stopped giving her that smile. Not when she'd broken him. Not when she'd confessed her infidelity and that she was in love with another man. Always, he smiled for her. Even when his eyes had been so full of pain she'd thought she'd drown in it. Still, he gave her that smile and his blessing.

She cringed away from the memory.

"Hi," she said, not knowing what else to say.

"Lance didn't want to come?"

Of course that would be first. Might as well get it out of the way. "Lance and I are no longer together."

"I'm sorry, Gwen." He was so sincere.

That was the shit of it. He *was* sorry. Noble bastard. "It's

97

okay. It's been over for a long time. We just hadn't gotten around to burying the corpse, you know?"

"Do you want to talk about it?"

"Not really." She shook her head. "Elaine pounced on me as soon as I stepped foot out the door and you know how she is."

Arthur wrinkled his nose. "That woman's mouth never stops."

"I was a little harsher than I needed to be, but I just want to be left alone. She's gossiped about me for hundreds of years. You'd think she be sick of me by now. I'm really not that interesting."

"You'll always be interesting to her, Gwen." Arthur led her inside. "You had what she wanted and she'll never understand why he chose you instead. She'll analyze everything about you from the way you wear your hair to that one crooked tooth."

"My teeth aren't crooked." Gwen slapped a hand over her mouth.

Arthur laughed, but didn't say anything else.

She wondered briefly if he knew what was going through Elaine's head because that's what had gone through his own when she'd chosen Lance. The very idea made her insides brittle and frail.

She had to stop this. She couldn't live in the past. It was over. If he wasn't bringing up the past, why couldn't Gwen leave it alone?

"What do you say we have dessert first?" He led her into a small salon and then from there, out onto a gorgeous veranda she didn't remember.

"This is new." She looked around to take in everything he'd added to that part of the castle.

"Time brings change to everything. Even Avalon."

There was a small table covered in white linen and a bowl of what looked like her precious gelato.

"Is that…" she began hopefully.

"It is. I heard you were a little upset that the market was out."

"How did you get it?" Gwen narrowed her eyes.

"I bribed a fairy."

"I could kiss you!" she blurted and then closed her eyes at the great, big pile of crap she'd just stepped in. Number one, he was her ex-husband. Two, he was a manwhore who had women throwing themselves at him. Three, she was just pathetic.

"Yeah, you owe me. The fairy wanted a kiss instead of gold, so it's only fair. Pay up." He pointed at his cheek.

Gwen leaned in and pressed her lips softly against his smooth cheek. His goatee tickled her chin and she couldn't help but giggle.

For which she mentally slapped herself.

"Kissing him was totally worth it." He mouth quirked into a half-grin.

Gwen choked. "Him?"

Arthur shrugged as the half-grin bloomed into a smile. "Seems everyone is agog at my reputation."

"So, was there tongue?"

"Why, you want to watch?"

"Sure. I mean, all this manwhoring and everyone else gets a piece of the action. Why not me?" Oh, she should've just let it go and not said anything. Now she'd backed herself into a corner. Why was she even flirting with him? She needed someone to take a wet newspaper across her snout like a puppy that had shit on the floor. That's what she was doing, shitting all over the floor.

"Guinevere, my love, any time you'd like a piece of

anything, all you have to do is let me know. You've got a VIP ticket."

She blushed and not knowing how to respond said, "You still didn't tell me if there was tongue."

"No, there was no tongue. He just wanted the blessing of a king. He was playing some twisted treasure hunt game. I told him I'd trade him for the gelato." Arthur smiled again. "I know, it's nowhere near as racy as you were thinking."

He pulled out her chair for her and she sat down, quickly plunging her spoon into the gelato. She struggled not to use her spoon like a steam shovel, but she'd been craving it.

Soon her bowl was empty and he pushed his own toward her.

"No, no. I couldn't. It will go straight to my ass."

"I will enjoy watching you eat it much more than if I ate it myself. After I kissed a fairy for you, the least you can do is indulge me."

"Hey, I already kissed you."

"That wasn't really a kiss."

"You're the one that presented your cheek," she blurted.

"Didn't know anything else was an option." He raised a brow and for some reason, Gwen thought it was the sexiest thing she'd ever seen. "Oh look, it's melting. It's such a shame to waste all that creamy goodness." Arthur nudged the bowl again.

"You're really not going to eat it?" Yeah, she could shove more gelato in her mouth and she wouldn't have to remember what it was like to belong to him, to have him belong to her, and worse, remember that she never wanted him while he was hers.

"Not a bite."

Gwen couldn't resist. She needed either the gelato or an

orgasm. The gelato would have to do. Not that it was a punishment, the gelato was almost a religious experience for her every time it touched her tongue. When she was finished, she licked her lips and set the spoon down gently in the bowl with a sigh, after licking it clean.

"I have decided to make it a crime for the market to ever run out of gelato."

"You're the king. You could do that."

"Or I could make it a crime for anyone to give you gelato but me."

"Why would you do that?" She tilted her head to the side.

"Honestly?"

"I... yes. Of course, honestly. Why would I ask a question if I didn't want the answer?"

"I don't know how you'll feel about the answer."

"Well, it's built up now. Just tell me. Did I humiliate myself or something? Do I have a ring of chocolate around my mouth?" She started dabbing at her lips with a napkin. Something like that would be par for the course.

"No. What you did to that spoon was illegal in some countries."

"Sorry." She bit her lip.

"No, don't be sorry. Let me get you another bowl."

She thought for a moment about how vociferously she'd enjoyed the gelato and realized she'd practically fellated the spoon. Gwen blushed hard. "At least there's proof I didn't forget how." Hell, her tongue had staged a full on rebellion saying whatever popped into her head and after she'd just given it gelato. The traitor.

"That's not something you forget, Gwen."

"After a hundred years, I'm sure it's possible."

"Are you telling me that you and Lance..."

She held up her hands. "I shouldn't have said anything. I really don't want to talk about it, but I seem to blurt out whatever nonsense happens to be tra-la-laing through my head when I'm with you. "

"You know you can tell me anything. I'm not going to judge you. I was just surprised."

"Yeah, you had all the sex so there wasn't any left for us." Gwen made a lame attempt at a joke.

"Dance with me," he commanded.

Gwen found herself swept into his arms and she didn't have the heart to refuse him, not when he flashed her that Teflon grin—that ever present smile that shined through every shadow.

The strains of Airborne Toxic Event's *Sometime Around Midnight* started playing. She relaxed into his arms, surrendered to his tender guidance and he spun her around the white-tiled veranda.

Gwen remembered the first time she saw him, their wedding, and their wedding night. Memories slammed into her just like the lyrics of the song. Feral waves, discordant and wild. The arms that held her had been so strong, so sure. His voice had been clear and confident as he'd spoken his vows to her. He'd meant every word.

She'd spoken the words, too, and she'd betrayed him.

A single shudder echoed through her body with all the force of a bullet. She'd broken Arthur and Camelot. She knew in that moment, she deserved everything she got.

"I'm sorry," she whispered against his chest.

"For what, Gwen?" He stroked her hair.

"Everything."

"I forgave you both a long time ago."

"I haven't forgiven myself." She clung to him. "Why couldn't you be a bastard?" Gwen sniffled.

"Are you crying?" he asked softly.

"No," she mumbled.

He pulled back from her and tilted her chin up so she had to look at him. "Gwen."

She closed her eyes. He could always see through her so easily.

"Look at me, Guinevere."

She opened her eyes and fell into the pool of his gaze. It was a long way down, but she owed him this. If he wanted to see her pain, it was the very least she could do.

"Not a goddamn one of us on this shit island is worth even one of your tears. Not Lance, that's for damn sure. And certainly not me."

Gwen wanted to bury her face in his chest and hide away from everything she'd done. She wanted to believe him, but that was the problem. She'd believed she deserved more for so long that she'd failed to see what she'd had in both Lance and Arthur.

He cupped her face in his hands and kissed away a tear.

She would've twined her arms around his neck and taken everything he wanted to give, if not for the voice of Bimbo Number One.

"Arthur, I left my panties upstairs."

Her voice, her words, what Gwen was doing in Arthur's arms, it was all like a bucket of cold water.

Gwen felt like she was trapped in the oncoming path of a runaway semi.

"Sorry, didn't know you'd already have more company or I would've called." Bimbo Number One grinned maliciously.

"I have to go," she squeaked. Gwen hated that she sounded like a mouse when she wanted to roar like a lion.

How could she have let herself forget he'd moved on?

This woman had more business here with him than Gwen did.

"Don't," he began.

She didn't even grab her shoes, but made a beeline for the stairs off the veranda and didn't stop until she was sure he couldn't see her. Then she crumpled in the grass like a new flower in a rainstorm and sobbed.

# CHAPTER
# THIRTEEN

MORGAN

Morgan woke up sticky, broken and confused.

She was on her back on the floor, with one leg propped up on the couch, the other hooked around part of the broken coffee table, one arm lying in a discarded hot wing plate, and she didn't even want to think about what she'd gotten in her hair.

She was naked.

There was still pie filling on one of her nipples.

Because Lance had wanted to lick it off.

A slow, lazy and satisfied smile curved her lips. She'd just banged the hell right out of Lancelot du Lac.

Best sex of her life, hands down.

She grimaced as she sat up, her girly bits ungrateful at their thorough use. Morgan would be lucky if she could walk, but that was a good thing. She'd think about Lance with every step she took and it would cement the memory of their time together in her head.

Morgan got to her feet gingerly and wondered if Lance

was already gone. She wouldn't blame him for sneaking out at first light. It's what she'd do in his position. When she heard his heavy gait in the hall, she realized she should've known better. That wasn't his style.

Thank the Goddess for magick; she didn't want him to see her like this. Or the living room. She snapped her fingers and the mess disappeared, her nakedness was covered by a filmy white sarong and her hair lay neat, shiny, and clean. Morgan zapped herself an instant mani/pedi for good measure.

When he came in, she saw he'd made use of the shower. His golden hair was damp and hung in a rebellious sweep over his forehead. He smelled of her honeysuckle conditioner.

Something about that made her want to pounce on him.

"So, is it out of your system?"

She remembered she'd told him she wanted to stay until she got him out of her system. If he left it up to her, she'd keep him forever. "Not a chance."

"Just thinking about last night, Morgan, I wanted to do it all over again." He grimaced.

"Stings, does it?" She closed the distance between them; sure of herself now that he'd admitted he wanted her again.

He grabbed her and jerked her against his hard chest. "Witch, you won't be smirking like the cat in the cream when you're screaming my name again."

"What's that about cream and cats?" she purred, flicking her tongue against the edge of his lip.

"You're going to kill me, Morgan, but I'll die happy."

She laughed. "We need to take a swim at the resort, lover. There's a certain type of seaweed that only grows near Avalon. I can make a healing tincture that will stand up to any and all *activity*."

He studied her for a moment and a serious expression clouded his face.

"None of that," Morgan spun away from him. "No excuses, no regrets. If you don't want to be here, just say so. Otherwise, let's just enjoy each other until it's over."

"I don't want to hurt you," he said quietly.

"Lance," she began as she headed out the door barefooted, "you'd have to have my permission to hurt me and I don't give it. So none of that knight in shining bullshit, okay? I'm an Evil Enchantress, remember?"

"You are definitely an enchantress, but there's not an evil bone in your delectable body." He followed her down to the beach.

"Up until yesterday, you were convinced I was the devil incarnate."

"No, I wasn't. I was just angry you made my dick hard."

She laughed again, feeling incredibly stupid that his words made her so happy. His wasn't the first dick she'd made hard and she doubted it would be the last. It was just a stupid, although sometimes delightful, biological function.

"Hmm, if you're still angry it sounds like I could be in for some good grudge sex." She jogged out in front of him on the wooden walk. "Maybe the marauding knight needs to pillage the maiden fair. If he can catch her."

"Would you like that, Morgan? You want me to bend you to my will?" He arched a brow.

"If you think you're man enough."

"Right now, I'd love to say I am, but I'm just talking shit until you mix up some of that tincture."

"I like a man who knows his own limits. And honestly, me too. It hurts to walk."

His chest puffed up like an inflated blowfish at her confession. "I made that."

"Yeah, you did." The look of pride on his face was one she hadn't seen for a long time. It pleased her to know she'd put it there.

"One more serious question and I promise, I'll let it go."

"We already let it go back in the living room, Lance."

"Come on. Just one." He grabbed her hand, his fingers warm and strong around her palm.

"What'll you give me for it?" She cast him a sly look from the corner of her eye.

"Anything you want."

"You know it's dangerous to make an open ended deal with a magickal being."

"I trust you."

"Your mistake." She didn't want him to trust her. It would make it all the more painful when this was over.

"So, it's a deal?"

"Fine. But you owe me the goods as stated: anything I want."

"So noted."

"Your serious, mood killer, downer question was?" she prompted. She knew this was going to be something else she didn't want to think about, but just as she couldn't change who she was, she couldn't change who Lance was either. And she didn't want to.

He laughed. "Do you think I should get a room at the inn?"

"Why?" She put her hands on her hips.

"Because I don't have anywhere to live and I don't want to take advantage of you. I don't want the Lane gossiping about how I moved right in with you when I left Gwen. Neither of you need that."

"Okay, one more time and I'll use small words so it sinks in. I know I'm the rebound. I know that staying with me isn't going to be a long term proposition. I didn't ask it of you. I liked waking up and having you close for easy access. If you don't want to sleep in the same bed because it's too intimate, I have a guest bedroom that yours to use even if you don't want to fuck me. And I don't give a blue-balled fairy fuck what anyone on the Lane has to say about me or the sainted Guinevere. Is that plain enough for you?"

"Yes, ma'am." He looked a little gobsmacked.

"Was it too plain? Did sweet little Gwen never say words like fuck?"

"She said them plenty, but she was never this assertive."

"Oh, so maybe instead of the pillaging the innocent maiden game, I should play up the wicked witch aspect a little more? Tie you up?"

"Morgan," he rumbled.

"Yes?" she replied sweetly.

"I already told you I'd like that."

"You did, didn't you?" she teased. "Maybe I'll have a pet knight, walk you around on a chain and beat that sweet ass of yours when you disobey me."

"That might be a bridge too far."

"Too bad. Pet knight isn't in charge. *I* am. You can call me Mistress."

The palm of his hand connected with her ass and Morgan found she quite liked it. "Too big for your britches, little witch."

"You know you like it. Makes your sword all... *battle ready*." She laughed again. Morgan realized she hadn't laughed this much in a long time. Morgan took the opportunity to smack his ass in return and was pleased with the sensation. He had a great ass. "Mm, that's Mistress Witch to you."

"We'll see about that."

Morgan found herself flat on her back in the sand, with Lancelot holding her wrists above her head with one hand. She shivered in delight, but then winced as her bits protested. "As romantic as sex on the beach sounds in stories, I don't want sand up my ass."

"Maybe chivalry isn't dead." He rolled, taking her with him so that he reversed their positions and she was astride him.

"Now that's romance. You'd take the sand up the ass for me." She leaned down and brushed her lips over his.

Images of forever started playing in her head like some morbid puppet show. She reminded herself that the ending to this story hadn't changed.

"Ready for a swim?" She scrambled off of him and began peeling her dress off to give him a show.

There was another reason she wanted the seaweed. Not only did it make a fantastic tincture to make the body forget its pain, it could make the heart forget, too.

Morgan knew she was going to need it.

# CHAPTER
# FOURTEEN

APHRODITE

For all intents and purposes, Aphrodite, the Goddess of Love, had been stood up.

The night had passed with no Rosa Regale and no hot welsh war god. If he didn't want to come over, he could've just said so. She hadn't read him wrong. He'd been as attracted to her as she was to him.

Unless her magick was off, which was possible because... because of Ares. Everything was his fault.

Her eyes widened. What if Aeron hadn't been as interested in her as she'd been in him? Aphrodite accepted the fact that not everything with a dick had a hard on for her. She was okay with that, but seeing as how her realm of influence was love and lust, if she chose to inspire those feelings, they should be felt, damn it.

Then she wondered if something had happened to him, and then hoped that it had. His only excuse for not showing up was that he'd been hit by a bus when he went to the mortal world to get her that bottle of Rosa Regale.

111

Yes, that was it. Hit by a bus, and then someone dropped an anvil on his head like in all of those Looney Tunes cartoons.

Because if he'd stood her up on purpose, she'd drop a mountain on him and his countrymen. His whole pantheon, this whole stupid island...

Well, she'd let Artemis and Morgan leave first, but the rest of them could go straight to Tartarus and—*Artemis.*

She sent out tendrils of her power to check on the other goddess and discovered things were progressing rapidly. Artemis had spent the night cuddling the bad boy of Avalon.

Aphrodite snickered. Vivienne's curse had been triggered, so they must have kissed. She wondered how long it would be before they came knocking on her door asking her to lift it?

Not until Artemis lost her V-card, that was for sure. That thing had to be gathering dust by now.

Something else tickled her power. It was Morgan. She planned to thwart Love. For some reason, this didn't piss her off like Vivienne's machinations did. Probably because Morgan wasn't a complete tool.

It didn't matter anyway. Morgan could rail against her future all she liked. It was fated. It would happen. It would've happened already if not for Guinevere.

Speaking of Guinevere—by Zeus this island was a hot spot for Love. There were so many hookups and entanglements that Aphrodite had been pinged in the head by her own power twice since she'd been here. Not very relaxing.

"How was your evening?" Ares said, materializing behind her.

Aphrodite considered lying and telling him that she'd

had the night of her life, but he was far too smug. He was up to something. "First of all, I told you we're on a break."

"It's a shame, Aphrodite."

"What is?" She wandered out onto the deck and slipped her feet into the water.

He followed. "That you're out chasing a god who can't even be bothered to show up when you've got me waiting for you. Even when you're angry with me, I don't want to be apart from you."

"How do you know what Aeron did or did not do?" Her tone was flip. "Unless you were out warmongering together and then you'd be in the same boat he's in. Maybe you should fuck each other and just leave me out of it?" She flicked her fingers in the water and debated a swim. Or drowning Ares, she hadn't decided.

"He stood you up. Isn't that enough reason not to see him again?"

"Again, how do you know?" Aphrodite looked up at him. "What did you do?"

Ares's face was suddenly the picture of innocence, which they both knew was a rancid lie.

"I may have told his pantheon if he kept his date with you Olympus and Asgard would smite them."

"You *what*?"

"Oh, come on, Aphrodite. If one little, insignificant threat was enough to deter him, he's not god enough for you anyway. I mean, really. Aren't you used to great deeds for love and all that rot? This is my great deed." He looked pleased with himself.

"I didn't want a great deed, dumbass. I just wanted you to say you love me."

"Same thing." He shrugged.

"So say it. Say those three words right now and I'll surrender."

He scowled.

"The answer is still go fuck yourself because you won't be fucking me." She eyed him and for the first time, Aphrodite dared to use her power to look into Ares's heart.

If he loved her and this was just another of his one-upmanship, she could let this one go and let him speak of his feelings in his own time. Even if that was another millennia.

She took a deep breath to gird herself for what she'd find.

Or worse, what she wouldn't.

Fearing there was nothing there for her had kept her curiosity at bay—until now. She was tired of the games, tired of the constant contest, just tired. She wanted to be loved wholly and completely.

After peering inside his heart, she saw the truth.

He was the embodiment of the worst Meatloaf song ever.

Ares wanted her.

Ares needed her.

But he wasn't ever going to love her.

All of the fight drained out of her at the realization, and she was flooded with other emotions. Fury at herself for being so weak and pathetic she hadn't looked before now. Sadness that this was over. All the dreams she'd ever had of a happily ever after with him were dust and ash. He'd been a key part of her life for eons.

He knew just where and how to touch her. He made her laugh. He protected her.

Yet it still came back to the fact that Ares wasn't in love

with her. She was something shiny to be kept on the mantle.

She took a deep breath and uttered the words that would change her life irrevocably. "Ares, it's done."

"What do you mean, *it's done*?" He sneered.

"Us. This. We're over." She died a little, speaking it out loud.

"For fuck's sake, Aphrodite. You're overreacting. This is par for the course for us." He took her hand.

"Ares," she thundered.

"Oh, I like it when you play rough."

"I'm not playing. I mean it. Do you want to know why?"

"I assume you're going to tell me whether I wanted you to or not." He sighed.

"Because you don't love me."

"Look, just because I'm not big on saying all that sappy shit doesn't mean—"

"*Ares*!" she snapped again.

"*What*!"

"It's not just about telling me that you love me. You. Don't. Love. Me."

"How do you know that? You're not me. You don't know what I feel."

"But I do," she whispered. "Because I looked." If she hadn't, Aphrodite might have actually believed that she'd hurt his feelings.

"You must have your wires crossed, woman, because I do love you, okay? Fine. There. I said it, you wretched harpy. *I love you*. Are you happy?"

"No. Because it's a lie. You just don't want your pretty toy to leave. You want to get tired of me first."

"You have officially lost your mind." He peered at her

like she was some foul stink bug he'd squished under his boot heel.

"If you just give it a chance, you'll see. Do you think I want it to be over? You're the father of my children. Well, most of them." She bit her lip as tears threatened. "You were my forever, but I'm not yours."

"You know what? You're right. We definitely need a break. I don't know what maggot has buried itself in your brain, but I can't deal with you until you dig it out. I gave you what you wanted and you're still not happy. Have you ever thought that maybe it's not about whether I love you or not, but if you're willing to accept my love? I'm not the promises and poetry type. You knew that when we started this. I'll fill your temple with sacrifices of flesh and blood, that's more my speed. I don't think you really love *me*. You love the idea of me. Turn that power on yourself and see what you find."

"Ares—"

"So you do whatever the hell you want. I'm going back to Olympus. I'll see you when I see you."

He disappeared.

Or at least she thought he'd disappeared. A heavy gait made the wooden boards creak and she flung a fireball. "I said—"

"I surrender!" Aeron caught the fireball and doused it in the clear, blue water that lapped at the edge of the dock.

Aphrodite blushed. "Oh, I'm sorry. That's twice I've smote you."

"You definitely have a temper." He seemed more amused than anything.

Aphrodite found that irritated her. He should respect her wrath. "You know what? You had that coming anyway for standing me up."

"Uh, did you not hear the part about the international incident and taking Avalon to war? Do you think one night with you is worth that?"

She lifted her chin. "As a matter of fact, I do." But her lip trembled.

The corner of his mouth turned up in a lopsided grin. "I do too, that's why I'm here."

To Aphrodite's absolute horror, she burst into tears. "Oh shit," she sniffed. "I'm sorry. I don't know what my problem is." She dashed at her cheeks with the back of her fists, sure she looked like minotaur crap. "That's not very attractive is it?" Aphrodite sniffed again. "I know you war types aren't comfortable with softer emotions."

"And why wouldn't we be?" He sat down next to her and hauled her up into his lap. "War is full of pain and sorrow. Loss." Aeron stroked her hair. "Love."

She turned her face against his neck and resisted the urge to compare him to Ares, or say what the other god of war would have done in this situation.

He knew what she was thinking anyway. "I told you, Ares is a dick. He's still very much a godling moving his action figures around on a chess board. He has yet to grasp the gravity of war."

His hands were so strong and sure as he held her that Aphrodite found herself leaning into his touch, and even though her heart was still full of Ares, she wanted more of Aeron.

"This, right now, it's not really worth taking Avalon to war. I'm sorry. I'll try to fix it with Ares."

He laughed. The sound rumbled low in his chest. "I'm not worried about it. Ares isn't going to do anything. My friend Morrigan can keep him occupied for the next hundred years or so."

Her power soared and she was struck with a vision of the future. It was of a small child with Ares's black hair toddling after a raven. The raven would stop, wait for the child to get close enough to pounce and then hop just out of reach.

But the raven wasn't actually a bird, it was Morrigan.

She was the child's mother.

*The goddess meant for Ares.*

The joy of seeding more love in the world bloomed inside of her, it fed her purpose, her *raison d'etre*, but it was soured by her own sorrow and her own loss. Ares was never meant to be hers.

It was really, truly, honestly over.

Aeron's arms tightened around her. "You saw something didn't you?"

Aphrodite choked on her own emotion, she couldn't speak.

"That's all right, *cariad*. It's all right." His voice was lyrical and soft in her ear and he made her believe it really would be okay.

"It's just, it's... I've told him it was over so many times, but I never believed it before now. It was never true. He's always been part of my life. Even when we were children."

"We were practice, Aphrodite. It was the same for Mori and I."

"We're a pair, aren't we?" She sniffed again.

"I suppose we could drown our sorrows together. I don't mind being the rebound god."

"You're not like anyone I've ever known, Aeron."

"How's that?"

"You accept everything so easily. You don't rail against Fate, or wallow in your pain. You simply bear it because it must be borne. Hades was much like you, but he felt everything all the way to his bones. You... you simply endure."

"I heard a rumor you tore his heart out of his chest."

"I did. Because he asked it of me." Aphrodite would never forget the proud god on his knees begging her to make the pain stop when he returned Persephone to the world above. She imagined that what she felt now was much like that. She'd released Ares to live the life he was meant to have.

"And if I asked?"

Aphrodite pulled away and looked up into his face, searching his eyes. She considered for a long moment before she spoke. "If that's what you need to heal, then yes. I'd do that for you."

"That's good to know, Aphrodite. Thank you."

"Did Morrigan hurt you that badly?" she asked softly.

"You could look and see."

She shook her head. "No, that's a violation. I won't look unless I need to. Do I need to?"

"No."

They sat in a companionable silence and Aphrodite found herself tracing the gryphon tattoo with her fingertips. A low sound that wasn't quite a growl rumbled from him.

"Ah, Aphrodite, *cariad*. He likes that much too well for you to continue."

"He?" she asked as his skin rippled under her touch.

"*Y Ddraig Goch,* the red dragon, and the protector of my people."

"But he's green."

"When he sleeps. If you touch him again, he will turn red and climb from my skin either to do battle or to take a mate. And that, my pretty Aphrodite is something you do not want."

She was intrigued. She couldn't help it. "But he's you. You talk about him like something different, a separate consciousness."

"He is, in a sense. Like your Lycanos. He is a beast without higher reasoning leashed only by my will."

Aphrodite's heart was sore, but her body was lonely and this god flipped every switch she had. Especially knowing that a primal beast lived under his skin—Aphrodite was drawn to him. She lived with love for a long time, she knew that she couldn't screw Ares out of her system, but maybe, just maybe, Aeron could make her forget for a little while. She shivered.

"Don't tell me you're afraid now."

"Oh no, Aeron." She licked her lips. "I'm not afraid." Aphrodite ghosted her fingers dangerously close to the tattoo. "Not afraid at all."

"What you are is playing with fire."

"So burn me."

"Aphrodite, things have changed."

She scrambled from his lap. "Are you serious? You were ready to come over and start a war just to fuck me, but now you don't want to? Are you trying to make me feel worse, because it's working," she snarled. "You just said you didn't mind being the rebound god."

"That was before you awakened the dragon. He wants you."

She put her hand on her hip. "Then I'm not seeing the problem."

"It took me years to get over Mori. I'm not afraid of love, obviously, but it's not fair to ask me to go into this knowing

I could fall in love when there's no chance of reciprocation on your part."

"Are you kidding me? You're... you're..." she stuttered. "You're a war god. You're not supposed to... damn it." Aphrodite stomped her foot.

"We're all vulnerable to love. Even War. Two sides of the same coin, isn't it?" he reminded her gently.

"What if I promise you that you won't fall in love? What if I swear it on my goddesshood?"

"I think Fate would smite you for daring to make such a promise."

"Why? Love is my realm and all things in it are subject to me. I have never had to work this hard to get laid."

"That's because I'm not that kind of god."

"Why, are you sick?" She was genuinely concerned.

"For a goddess of love, you seem to be rather ignorant in the ways of the heart."

But rather than be insulted, Aphrodite knew he was right. Too many years of trying to mold herself into what Ares wanted. Too many years of thinking he was the norm when the truth was he just didn't love her.

"Okay, I'll give you that one. You're right. I don't know how I'm supposed to act, or what to expect. But don't you think I should learn?"

"Two rules. Don't touch the dragon—"

"Never had a man or a god tell me that before," she snickered.

He flashed a smirk. "Yeah, well, there's the dragon. And then there's *the dragon*."

"So which one am I allowed to touch?" She gave him the most innocent expression she could muster.

"Neither one."

She narrowed her eyes.

"Not on the first date."

"You haven't even asked me out yet."

"Nope." And with that, he disappeared, leaving Aphrodite more frustrated than ever.

"I should swear off war gods. I really should," she muttered aloud.

She could call Poseidon. He was all about the manwhoring. He'd be the first one to say the way to get over one god was to get *under* another. She heard he did delightful things with that trident.

# FIFTEEN

VIVIENNE

Vivienne's power had never been stronger. When she awoke the next day, it was with the sun and all the green and growing things that surrounded her cottage were bright and verdant. Roses had even started to climb the trellis again.

And she'd never felt as guilty either.

She and guilt were good friends, but moaning Arthur's name with her legs wrapped around Hector de Maris had to be the rotten jewel in a twisted crown.

Hector had to have heard her, but he made no mention of it, gallant creature that he was.

She was wholly unworthy.

His words echoed in her ears.

*"I'll be your confessor, Vivienne. I'll keep your sins."* When she'd confessed her sin, and that she didn't and couldn't love him, his words stabbed even deeper. *"That's my penance for lust. Coming on my cock instead of his is yours."*

She bit her lip and closed her eyes, taking a deep breath to steady herself because come on his cock she certainly had and moaning Arthur's name aside, she wanted to do it again.

Vivienne wondered if she could summon him to her door and—and then what? Demand he fulfill his duty? No. It happened, but it couldn't happen again. Maybe it was time for her to finally confess everything to Arthur so she could move on with her life.

That was completely selfish. He could probably go the rest of his existence without knowing exactly why Vivienne had screwed him over. Her urge to confess was simply to allay her guilty conscience so she could finally move on.

But no, this was hers to bear. She'd wrought it, she had to live with it.

A loud banging echoed through her little cottage like gunshots.

She was both surprised, thrilled, and embarrassed all at once to see Hector standing at her door. Memories of the previous day washed over her yet again, how his strong hands felt roving her body, the way his muscles moved while he drilled into her, and the taste of his mouth.

Her cheeks were suddenly hot and she felt like a maiden again—the sensation completely at odds with the dirty thoughts she currently indulged.

"Hello," she said, her hair falling across her cheek.

"Are you well then, Vivienne?"

"Fully restored, thank you." Goddess, how pathetic was that? She'd just thanked him for shagging her.

An awkward silence crashed between them like a meteor, but neither would mention it.

"Would you like to come in for some apple ale?" She

held the door wider, trying not to stare as the sun's rays seemed to halo him and glint off his golden hair.

How had she missed it? Hector de Maris was more beautiful than any of the gods she'd ever seen on Avalon. This had to be a dream. Hector couldn't possibly want her. When he said he'd lusted, maybe he lusted for another and he thought—

"I'd like that very much."

His voice short-circuited the route of rational thought and she stood there, dumbstruck.

This had to be some kind of spell. Her reaction to him wasn't natural. In all the years they'd been on Avalon, she'd never noticed him like this.

She fumbled around until she found the ale and using her magick, she chilled it at just the right temperature before handing him the bottle. Vivienne made it herself from Avalon's apples.

He took a long pull off the bottle and she was mesmerized by the movement of his mouth against the lip, the way his throat worked as he swallowed. "The best ale in the world is made on Avalon by your hands, Vivienne."

The heat in her cheeks intensified. "And who else's ale have you been drinking to know that, Sir Hector?" She tried to sound like she was admonishing him, but it came out sex-kitten deluxe instead.

"Everyone's." He winked and if she'd been wearing panties, they would've melted right off her. "Lance and I used to party with Dionysus. He'd pick us up and we'd go on a mortal pub crawl from Ireland to Santa Monica."

"Really? For some reason, I thought you'd never left Avalon."

"That was the image I wanted you to have of me, Vivienne. I'm glad all my hard work paid off. I wanted to be the

125

best and brightest of your guard. I thought you'd notice me."

The smile he wore pained her. It wasn't really a smile, but more of an expression of hopeless acceptance. What had she done?

"I used to be angry with you."

Rather than be offended, Vivienne accepted she'd done him a great wrong. She knew that. By ignoring her guard, she'd not provided them with what they needed either. She could see that now. "What else did I do besides neglect my duty?" Vivenne asked softly, inviting him to release his burden.

"I was still a child then. I had these grand dreams that when I joined your guard, you would choose me as you did yesterday. I was angry when you didn't and I betrayed my vows every time I left Avalon."

"Why are you telling me this now?" She considered all the feelings that roiled through her and she realized this was a similar situation to what transpired between her and Arthur.

"Because you finally did choose me and I wasn't worthy. That's really why I came. I wasn't pure. I wanted to make sure there were no ill effects and your magic wasn't corrupted."

She laughed and it was a cold, bitter noise that erupted from an icy place inside of her. "Oh, Hector." Vivienne reached up to touch his cheek. "If anyone is corrupt or unworthy, it's me. I coveted and lusted too. I sinned. In punishing myself, I was punishing you. I didn't acknowledge or accept your sacrifice or your service. Can you forgive me?"

His large hand closed over her wrist and he turned his face into her palm. Vivienne was humbled by the action.

She felt very small and feminine, but infinitely powerful at the same time.

"Only if you forgive yourself," he answered.

"I don't know how."

"Start by acknowledging that even though you are the venerable Lady of the Lake, you're still a woman." He dropped her hand. "Even the goddesses who come here on holiday admit that."

"I think I admitted that very well yesterday." She pursed her lips as a blush crept over her cheeks.

"No, you didn't. You denied it like it was something dirty. You are the Lady of the Lake, not a Catholic nun. You didn't marry your god, you love him in a much more earthy way. And you were meant to."

"Couldn't you apply the same reasoning to yourself?"

"No." He shook his head. "I took a vow to remain chaste and I did not."

"I release you from that vow, Hector." As she said the words, something inside of her changed. It *hurt*.

"Then I vow it again, because I am the last. There is no male energy to feed you, Lady, without it." Hector fell to his knees. "Will you have my vow?"

"No," Vivienne cried. "It's—" Wrenching pain twisted her gut.

"I am the last, there cannot be ying without yang. I know I'm not worthy, but I'm all that's left."

Goddess, how could he think he was unworthy?

*Because that's what you've taught him with your neglect.*

Another wave of pain washed over her, like her bones were trying to climb out of her skin. She'd only ever felt this once before and that was when she'd risen from initiate to Lady of the Lake.

In her guilt, she'd neglected her duties to everyone.

How could she ever begin to forgive herself? These were her transgressions, not feelings for a man who didn't return them.

If anyone was unworthy, it was Vivienne. She had not served her office or the people who depended on her.

A boom of thunder cracked and lightning struck, the small cottage burst into flames around them and Vivienne was consumed.

Electricity jolted through her and as it receded, it took her magick with it.

When it finally released her, Vivienne was Lady of the Lake no more.

# CHAPTER
# SIXTEEN

ARTEMIS

An exclamation of "son of a bitch" was certainly not what Artemis expected to hear after she kissed Bad Boy Extraordinaire Mordred Le Fey. Neither was him tucking her in to bed next to him like a five year old who wouldn't be still for naptime.

Even worse was that she'd fallen asleep rather than demanding an explanation along the lines of: "What the actual fuck?"

And worse than that, she'd awakened to his fingers pushing her hair away from her face and she'd liked it. Not just enjoyed it, but had stupid thoughts about how she wouldn't mind waking up like this for the *rest of her existence.*

Bad. Bad. Bad.

Apparently, he thought the same thing. "Son of a bitch," he said it again.

"Look—" she rubbed her eyes "—you've got to stop saying that or you're going to give me a complex."

"You?" He blinked his gorgeous eyes. "I'm the one who was cursed yesterday."

"Oh really?" Artemis rolled over on her side and propped her head up on her hand. "Tell me more."

"It's a right bitch of a curse, too."

Artemis's eyes widened. "Oh my Goddess! It was you! You're the one who was the brunt of the curse that got Aphrodite's toga in a wad!"

"Aphrodite is on Avalon?"

Artemis nodded. "She and Ares are on a break. So we decided on girls' getaway."

His eyes narrowed. "So why are you in my house and not in a cabin with her at the resort?"

Artemis considered for a moment. "Why don't you tell me about your curse first?"

She expected him to balk, but he didn't. "I may have played a prank on Vivienne that she didn't care for, so to punish me, she cursed me to fall in love with the next woman I kissed."

Artemis's heart skipped a beat. "Well, I kissed you, you didn't kiss me, so you should be fine."

"Woman, I don't know where you were for that encounter, but I most definitely kissed you back."

"I didn't notice. I was too nervous. That was my first kiss."

"You know, this might not be too bad of a deal." Mordred twined a lock of her hair around his finger.

"How can you say that? It's horrible." Except she was mesmerized by the way her hair curled freely around his flesh and she wondered what it would feel like if she could curl her body around his in the same way.

He smile turned predatory. "I know you're here because you want me to be your first. It's not a new ploy, although you're the first one my mother has thrown my direction."

Hair twirling aside, "Thrown your direction? Like I'm a fucking dog bone?"

"I didn't say that and really, you have to understand, after centuries of being a theme park attraction, one tends to think of these things in a bit more callous way."

Artemis supposed she could see it from his point of view. She hated feeling like all anyone wanted from her was to be the first to get between her thighs, like she had no other value aside from that.

"But this is good for you because when you fall in love with me, I'll already love you back."

All softer thoughts and empathy for him fled. "You're a pig." She tugged her hair away from his grasp. "You assume just because I may have wanted you to be my first that I'm going to fall in love? As childbirth is in my realm, as I've told you before, I've seen the difference between sex and love many times. One doesn't always equal the other and nor should it. So you think just because you might have some skill in the bedroom, I'll love you? Love is about more than pleasure. Did it ever occur to you that women choose you because you're a throwaway?"

As soon as it was out of her mouth, she regretted it. That was a horrible thing to say, but his smug expression coupled with the assumption that just because she was a virgin she'd be arrow over quiver for him was ridiculous and insulting.

"Artemis, I have no doubt that's why *every* woman chooses me. I've been a throwaway, as you so kindly put it, since my conception. My mother never wanted a child, she bore me because it was her duty to Avalon. When I brought down Camelot, the world had no other use for me. I was a throwaway, just as you said. Fucking is what I'm good for. I'm under no illusions about that, sweetheart." He purred sweetheart like it was insult rather than an endearment. "And yet, the women who want my touch do fall in love anyway, for some fucking reason. They all think they'll be the ones to fix me, the one I'll change for."

"That sounds miserable. I'm sorry." Artemis couldn't imagine living like that, knowing she wasn't good for anything but sex. Or a weapon. An object to be used. That was why she'd wanted to stay a virgin forever. She wanted someone to see her value past a womb. And now she was doing the same thing to someone else.

The bitterness in his voice was gone as quickly as it had come. "Don't be sorry, just don't do it."

"Don't do what?" She arched a brow and pushed down her feelings. She wasn't sure if it was empathy or pity and she knew he wouldn't want either one.

"Don't fall in love."

"I won't. Aphrodite won't let me." She was secure in that. Aphrodite would never let her love someone who didn't love her back. "And we'll get her to lift Vivienne's curse, too. I promise."

"Why would you promise such a thing? What do you want in return?" He was wary, suddenly studying her as perhaps he would an angry skunk.

"I thought we'd established that already. I want you to punch my V-Card. I mean, since we're being honest and all that." She pursed her lips for a moment. "Yes, I have to say I like approaching this honestly much better."

"I don't. It was more fun when we were playing cat and mouse." His bottom lip plumped with what Artemis might call a pout.

It was adorable.

She suddenly had visions of him as a solemn-faced child with round cheeks and that shock of black hair. Of course he'd been spoiled absolutely rotten. Artemis couldn't imagine telling him no about anything. Morgan must have had a spine of steel to raise him to be even a poorly functioning adult.

"No one said we couldn't play games. At the risk of repeating myself, I am the Goddess of the Hunt, after all. I love games. I love the chase. But I'd rather be honest about my intentions."

He perked. "I like this development. I've always said the sharpest, most brutal weapon is the truth."

"Excellent. Can we get to the seducing now?" Her words were much bolder than how she actually felt. She did indeed want to get on with it, but there was a flutter of fear in her belly when she thought about what exactly getting on with it involved.

"It doesn't quite work like that."

"Why not?"

He cocked his head to the side as he considered. "Okay."

Mordred pounced on her like a hawk would a mouse and Artemis found herself pressed down in the bed, his heavy weight pinning her. She almost panicked, she'd been in this situation before when some of her petitioners had become too ardent and she'd been afraid, but the look on his face was playful and even though he behaved like some lithe predator, Artemis just knew he wouldn't hurt her.

Maybe because he was cursed to be in love with her, but her gut swore she could trust him.

"Relax your legs. Let me into your temple, Artemis."

If anyone else said it, she might have laughed, but there was just something about Mordred Le Fey that made everything the man said sound like sex on a stick. Let me into your temple? That was almost as bad as—

Every thought fell out of her head because as she opened for him, he was positioned so intimately against her she could feel the hard ridge of his cock rubbing against the thin silk of her panties.

Desire stabbed through her hot and sharp and she couldn't breathe, couldn't think, she could only feel. She was equal parts aroused and afraid.

"In for a penny, right love?" He crushed his mouth to hers and it was no tentative caress, no worshipful veneration. It was primal and earthy, dark and delicious, just like he was.

He tasted of dark, sweet things like red wine and ripe blackberries. She was surprised how hot his hands were, his skin was like marble and she expected his touch to be like cool stone, but he was all fire.

Artemis decided she could gladly burn in him.

She wrapped her legs around his waist, locking him against her with only the barest hint of silk keeping him from piercing her virginity.

She thought there would be more, exploring each other, tasting each other, but this was fairly straightforward and it took away a bit of the mystique. Artemis didn't think Mordred would have achieved his legendary lover status if this was all there was to it. There had to be more.

Not that what was happening wasn't nice, it was. Fireworks and all that, but there was supposed to be more than fireworks, like the births of universes and lots of that cosmic stuff. Or so she'd always heard.

"Artemis," he whispered against her ear. "Stop analyzing it and enjoy it."

"I just want to make sure I'm getting it right."

"It's about the moment, love. Surrender to it."

"I can't."

"Ah, I see. This is where the games come in. I do believe you just challenged me." His breath was warm against her ear, his lips brushed her skin.

"I believe I did." She shivered in anticipation.

He hooked his fingers around the edges of her panties and slid them down her legs, discarded them like a candy bar wrapper and dipped his head.

She grabbed him by the hair. "Uh, what are you doing?"

"What do you think I'm doing? I'm rising to the challenge." He mouth looked more wicked somehow so close to her bits.

"You can't mean to—"

"I most certainly do." He attempted to dip his head again, but she maintained her grip on his hair.

"You can't."

"Why not?" He studied her.

"You just can't. I mean… you can't."

"You are best friends with the Goddess of Love and you haven't heard about the delights of cunning linguists?"

"What does being multi-lingual have to do with it?" Artemis was confused.

"*Everything*, sweetheart. It's about how fast I can move my tongue." Instead of trying to get her to release his hair, he raised her hips and brought his meal to his mouth.

The first flick of his tongue and Artemis suddenly understood about galaxies and universes and supernovas, they were all born on the tip of Mordred Le Fey's tongue.

# CHAPTER
# SEVENTEEN

GWEN

She didn't want to answer the knock on the door. Gwen knew it was Arthur. She couldn't face him. If she could go the rest of eternity and never—no, that was a lie. Just the thought of never seeing him again was poison. She was hungry for the sight of him, the sound of his voice, and the warmth of his presence. There had always been something about him that filled up a room.

Some men sucked all of the air out of a space, some had a charisma that was magnetic, but Arthur was different. Instead of drawing everyone and everything to him, he filled up all the moments between breath—delving and twining himself inside until you didn't know where he ended and you began. It was how he inspired such greatness, such loyalty.

Gwen had resented it.

Now, she was so empty and lost, and he was true north.

Bittersweet didn't taste like she thought it would. Ashes and dust, maybe, with a pain that was like picking at a scab.

But no, it was more like an overripe apple, sweet and rancid, its juice bleeding with every bite.

"Gwen, I know you're in there. Are you really going to leave your king standing on your doorstep like a beggar?" He used his "royal" voice, the reverberation thundering through the door.

"I'm not well, Arthur."

"Bullshit. Open the door."

"As my lord commands," she snapped and flung the door open.

She knew she looked like utter crap, eyes red-rimmed and swollen from her crying jag the night previous. She hadn't brushed her hair and she was wearing the non-Yoga doing Yoga pants and a ratty t-shirt. In short, she was wallowing.

"I brought your shoes." He handed them to her by the straps.

"Thanks." She tried to close the door, but he braced his arm against the door and stepped inside.

"I'm sorry."

"*Oh my GOD!*" she shrieked. "What are you apologizing for?" How dare he apologize. How dare he be so fucking noble. It burned her more than any fire ever could.

"I wanted you to know I didn't plan on any company but you."

"Arthur, that's the least of what I deserve for what I did."

"I'd never hurt you, Gwen." He was so earnest.

She couldn't stand it, Gwen had no defenses against him. "Well, I beg to differ. There was that whole burning me at the stake thing." Yeah, she had to hold on to that or she'd break—shatter like a glass ball dropped on pavement.

"I knew Lance would save you."

"You couldn't be sure." *No, no... he couldn't. Could he? Oh God.*

Arthur flashed her a pained smile. "Yes, I could. That's the kind of man he was and the only way he'd leave with you. I just wanted you to be happy."

Yes, that same smile that shined for her no matter what she'd done. Arthur knew Lance even better than she ever had. Could any creature alive be so selfless? She couldn't face it—him. Even though Camelot was gone, even though he'd tried to muddy himself with meaningless encounters, he was still every bit the shining beacon of hope and goodness he'd been all those years ago.

"You're killing me," she whispered, the shoes falling from her hands and her knees went weak.

He was there, just like always, to catch her. His arms closed around her. "That's because I'm already dead, Gwen. I died when you left me."

Gwen hadn't thought words could cut any deeper, she didn't think there was any pain left to feel, but there was. It sprang an eternal fountain of sorrow scalding her insides.

"I'm nothing special." In that moment, she knew it was true. She'd been a queen, but that didn't matter. She shoveled herself into her too tight yoga pants like every other woman.

"You're always my Guinevere, my queen, my love. *Always.*"

It was like some law of inevitability had been enacted in that moment, she could no more stop herself from tilting her face up to his than she could turn the tide or blot out the sun.

He kissed her and his lips were like sugared razor blades —sweet and sharp. All her pain, all of her failure, all her shame welled like blood and spilled over her tongue. But she didn't stop the kiss, instead she surrendered to it and wherever he wanted to take her.

It was Arthur who broke the kiss and rested his forehead against hers. "Ah, Gwen. There's nothing in this world or the next I want more than you." His fingers were gentle on her cheek as he cupped her face. "But only if I'm really what you want. If you just need someone to cling to, someone to hold in the dark, I can't. I thought I could, but I can't."

He released her and for all intents and purposes, fled. He left her standing there in the door, watching him, without ever looking back.

Gwen's lips were swollen from his kiss, her body alive with the sparks of pleasure he'd wrought with his touch, his words.

But it was wrong.

She knew what she had to do.

Before she could change her mind, she shoved her feet into her tennis shoes and ran all the way to The Witch's Brew. She didn't let herself think about what she was doing as she ran, only that it was the right thing to do. She could do this, she could be the one who finally did the right thing.

"Morgan," she cried out as she barreled through the door, searching for the witch.

The other woman's eyes widened and she raised her hands ready to curse her.

Lance flung himself in front of her. "No, don't!"

She placed her hand on his shoulder, and stepped out from behind him. Honestly, it felt strange to touch him. Foreign, after being in Arthur's arms again. How quickly things changed—at least after they'd been acknowledged. Centuries they'd stayed together when there was nothing to hold them there.

"I did as you suggested, Lance. I asked Arthur for forgiveness. He's given it to me. Now, I need to give him something in return and I need Morgan to help me." She turned her attention back to the witch. "If you'd consider it."

Morgan looked around, peered out the window and then looked back at Gwen. "Well, it sure doesn't look like the apocalypse is upon us, but I've been wrong before."

"I deserve that and a lot more from you. I accept that. But Arthur doesn't. Please, will you hear what I have to say?"

"By all means. Come back to my office."

"Morgan, I really don't think—" Lance began.

"We didn't ask you." Gwen said in a soft voice, but there was no rancor.

"I'd like it noted for the record this is a bad idea."

"So noted," Morgan and Gwen said simultaneously.

Gwen realized that maybe she and Morgan were more alike than she'd imagined and she'd spent years hating her.

Morgan led her to a door and Gwen followed her inside.

"Well, you're either very brave or very stupid. Which is it?" Morgan said when they were seated at a small table.

"Probably very stupid." Gwen admitted.

Morgan narrowed her eyes. "You're really starting to freak me out. If you came because of Lance—"

"No. I said—oh." It just occurred to her why Morgan behaved as she had. She wasn't usually so quick on the draw and Lance was sure Morgan was going to curse her.

And he hadn't been afraid of Morgan.

He was *with* her.

Part of her wanted to be angry, but that part was the last remnant of the child she'd been. The child who'd fallen in love with a golden knight who was nothing short of a god. The child who was now relegated to a box of memories and simpler times.

Morgan studied her hard before speaking. "Goddess help me." She shook her head and sighed. "It's not serious between Lance and I. You'll probably work it out—"

"No." Gwen swallowed hard. Knowing the truth and speaking it were two different things, but not speaking it didn't change it. So she plunged ahead. "We won't work it out. It's been over for a long time. This is the way things were supposed to be, I think. Somewhere along the way, things got twisted up."

"I twisted them." Morgan confessed.

"Me too." Gwen felt another rush of kinship with the other woman and took her hand. "We all fucked up."

"You say fucked?"

"I say a lot of things."

"I always thought profanity would curl your hair." Morgan snorted.

"If it would just brush it, that would make me happy." She sighed heavily. "I ran all the way here. I wanted to do this before I chickened out."

"This must be heavy. What is it?"

"I want you to make a charm so Arthur won't love me anymore."

The silence was deafening.

"Why the hell would you want that?"

"I don't. But it's what's right." The words choked her.

"Why?"

"He's in pain. He still loves me after... everything."

"Okay, color me stupid, but you love him, too."

"Yes."

"Then what's the problem?"

"It's toxic, it's poison. He's still hurting after all of these years and what I did—loving him back won't heal those wounds. Only digging out the cancer, and that's me."

"Hell," Morgan exclaimed.

"Will you help me?" Gwen hated asking her, but it was finally time to do the right thing.

"I couldn't if I wanted to. I can do a lot, but my magick can't affect real love one way or the other. But there may be someone on the island who can help you. Aphrodite is here."

"Is she on vacation? Oh hell, is she here to see Arthur?" Gwen clenched her fists so tightly her nails dug into her palms.

"Actually, she brought her friend here to meet Mordred. But let's not worry about that right now. I'll take you to her."

"Thank you, Morgan." The cracks in her heart splintered a little more with every word she spoke.

"Are you sure this is what you want?"

"What do you mean?"

"Only that whatever Aphrodite does can't be undone. If you want her to pry you out of him, then you're gone and the way in is lost to you forever."

The final piece of her heart shattered, and that was how Gwen knew she was absolutely doing the right thing. "Yes."

# EIGHTEEN

MORGAN

Guinevere du Lac was stupid.

It was something Morgan had always suspected—dumber than a box of hair. That was the only explanation for the way that woman's brain worked.

Morgan knew that she herself was dumber than a box of hair when it came to love, too. After all, she'd fallen in love with a man who could never be hers, and like the dumbass she was, she'd settled for crumbs knowing it was going to break her heart when it was over. But if Lance could have ever loved her, Morgan wouldn't throw it away.

There was dumb and then there was too stupid to live.

"Aphrodite is down at the resort. I'll take you." Morgan didn't agree with what Guinevere wanted, but it wasn't her place to say so.

"Morgan?" Gwen said haltingly.

"What?" She studied the other woman as she wrung

her hands, the emotions that bloomed on her face and then wilted, only to bloom again.

"Thank you."

Morgan pursed her lips. They were never going to be besties, and it was hard to change the habits of centuries, but maybe they didn't have to hate each other anymore.

"You're welcome."

"Morgan?" she asked again.

"What now? Can't we just...you know...move this along?" Morgan cringed.

"You can have Lance."

She arched a brow in full on Evil Enchantress fashion. *Who was she to say*—Morgan reigned in her bitchkitty and exhaled heavily.

"What I mean to say is, I can see you already have him." Gwen bit her lip. "I just want you to know I don't begrudge either of you. If he can forgive you for what you did with Elaine and the potion, then I can, too. It's not my place to be angry. And if I'm being honest, I was always jealous of you."

Each of Gwen's words tore through her like bullets. "All of this honesty feels like a rash." Morgan shifted uncomfortably.

"You're telling me? Goddess, Morgan. I've stewed and frothed and hated you for so long because you always had what I wanted."

Morgan was sure she was going to fall over dead if Gwen kept talking. "Me? You married Arthur. You married Lance. You were always perfect little Guinevere who had to be protected, indulged—"

"And it was hell. I'd much rather have been a woman that men feared. I'd rather have been seen as strong, capable and in charge of my own destiny. You and Vivienne wrought kingdoms, crowned kings, and wrote history. What was I, but a well-born broodmare who couldn't even produce an heir?"

Something welled in Morgan that she didn't want to name. She always knew she was right, but somehow, it didn't feel good to be right. Damn. She'd fantasized about rubbing that in Gwen's face and now, she didn't want to. She didn't want Gwen to hurt any more than she already had.

That was an irritating development. Yes, very much like a rash.

"We destroyed kingdoms, too. We destroyed lives and hurt people." Morgan gestured, as if she could physically deflect those words before they made impact.

"So did I." Gwen looked down at her hands. "I destroyed two men who were the best that humanity had to offer. Look what I did to them, all because I needed to be loved. At least you were trying to change the world. I was only trying to change *my* world."

Empathy for the Bitch Queen was the last thing Morgan ever wanted to feel. It was even worse, like chigger bites in a no-no place, than admitting she was in love with Lance.

"Look, it's not for me to forgive you." She sighed. "Or judge you. The powers that be do as they will and their reasons are their own. Oftentimes, it's not meant for us to know. Arthur and Lance both played their own parts in what happened. Own what you did, but you can't take the blame for everything."

"I really want to hug you, but I don't want you to turn me into a frog." Gwen bit her lip.

"Fuck it." Morgan hugged her tight.

And the world didn't explode. Fancy that.

A knock echoed through the door. "It's too quiet in

there. You guys are either killing each other, or making out." In a quieter voice he said, "If you're making out, I want to watch."

Morgan and Gwen jerked apart and Gwen tittered a high-pitched giggle.

"Yeah. The best humanity has to offer and he wants to know if we're making out." Morgan snorted.

"That's because I told him about my handmaiden, Brigid."

Morgan almost choked. "Excuse me?"

Gwen shrugged. "It was her duty to see to *all* of my needs. Marrying a warlord, as Arthur was at the time of our marriage, meant he'd be gone on campaign. A lot. Lance really liked those stories." She pursed her lips. "Once upon a time, anyway."

It occurred to Morgan, for the first time, that Guinevere was a flesh and blood woman with wants, needs, and hopes. That maybe, just maybe, even she was allowed to make mistakes, too.

Morgan hated learning these kinds of lessons. It meant all that time she'd spent hating her had been wasted. Of course, she knew it would be, but at the time, she wasn't feeling very enlightened.

Words she hadn't wanted to say bubbled up like a crap stew and they tasted just as horrible, but out they came anyway. "I'm sorry, Gwen."

"For what?"

"For being jealous of you, too. For wishing bad things on you and it seems like your plate was already really full."

"I'm coming in." Lance growled.

The wicked witch in her was tempted to lock the door and wait for him to try to break it down and then open it and watch him sprawl ass over teacakes into the room. It would be funny, but he sounded genuinely concerned. So she opened the door.

"Who are you worried about? Me or her?"

His eyes were wide, and it was clear from the look on his face that he wasn't sure what the right answer was.

"Uh, both of you."

"Really?" Morgan put a hand on her hip.

"No, it was me. But only because he was sure you'd turn me into a frog."

"That's the third reference to a frog. I have never, in my life, turned anyone into a frog." Morgan was indignant.

"I seem to recall that knight who got a little too handsy," Guinevere began.

"I didn't turn him into a frog. It was a milking cow to see how he liked having his "teats" yanked on all the time. But no, it was never a frog."

"That's exactly what I meant, Morgan. He's not worried about you because you're powerful."

"She's a sorceress. I'd worry about *me* if I pissed her off." Lance was emphatic.

Morgan didn't like that at all. She didn't want him to fear her. It made her think that he was afraid of her—that maybe what was happening between them now was because he'd started something he didn't know how to end.

Occam's Razor said that the simplest answer was usually the right one. How likely was it that Lancelot du Lac, the knight in literal shining armor had always had a secret *tendre* for the court witch, centuries he'd wanted her, fantasized about her, but never had the courage to tell her? This man who slayed dragons? Or maybe, he'd just gotten drunk after splitting with his wife and Morgan had been warm and willing. But now he didn't know how to—

Hell. If he'd actually slayed a dragon he shouldn't be afraid of her.

But that little niggling voice of doubt wouldn't shut its stupid cakehole.

"Well, obviously everything is fine. Gwen is in one, human piece. I'm going to take her down to see Aphrodite."

Gwen looked back and forth between them, and said, "I'll just wait for you outside." She put her hand on Lance's shoulder, squeezed and walked out.

"What the hell was that? She went from telling me to burn in hell to being my wingman." His shook his head, disbelief written on his features. "I don't get it."

"Maybe she was worried I'd turn *you* into a frog," she sneered.

"Morgan, come on. You know I'm not afraid of you. I know you two don't like each other and even though Gwen and I aren't together anymore, she doesn't deserve warts or any other magickal plague."

Morgan was torn. Part of her applauded that he was still Gwen's champion, but the selfish part of her, the one where that little voice resided, it wondered if there would ever be a day when he wasn't the Queen's Champion.

Even as she wondered, she knew the answer. She'd known it before they started this. Lancelot du Lac would never be Morgan's. He'd always belong to something brighter, something more pure. Something good.

"We talked. She's fine. I'm fine, too, in case you were worried."

"Morgan, you'd crush her like a bug. Evil Enchantresses don't need champions." Lance cocked his head to the side and flashed her a grin.

"Hmm." She pursed her lips. She'd been doing that so often lately, she wondered if it was going to give her wrinkles. "You think we don't? Maybe we don't need them, but maybe we want them."

The grin melted off his face. "Morgan, if you want something from me, you need to just tell me what it is." Lance was so earnest, as always.

But Morgan found she couldn't answer him. Her pride wouldn't let her because it knew how this would go down. He would tell her all the things he couldn't give her, he'd apologize for not being able to love her—no. She would never reach so high he'd have to slap her hand.

"No, I don't want anything from you." She grinned. "Well, maybe that's not the whole truth. I want your cock."

"You can have that as many times as you'll put up with it." Lance grabbed her and pulled her close.

They were back in comfortable territory now, no feelings, no softer things. Just sex. Just the friction between their bodies—the all-consuming heat that incinerated them both.

"When I get back?" She rubbed her cheek against his, kneaded her nails lightly into his shoulders.

"Any time you want, Wicked Witch."

The evidence of his arousal was hard against her belly and she imagined having him take her right there. Again, that bad part of her, it liked that he'd fuck her while his ex-wife was waiting.

But Gwen had asked her for help and Morgan was more than a witch, a sorceress, or any of the other names that they called her. She was a servant of Avalon. When its denizens were in need, it was up to Vivienne and Morgan to answer their call as best they could.

"I'll be back soon." She brushed her lips over his.

"Try not to drown her on the way, okay?"

His concern irritated her like steel wool panties. "Lance,

again, with the small words so you can understand. Gwen came to me for help. I'm sort of magickally bound to help her. It's in my job description, but don't let that get out or I'll have all manner of people up my broomstick about stupid shit they could fix themselves. Gwen can't fix this herself. And she's perfectly—" Morgan paused. She didn't want to lie. "—mostly safe with me," Morgan corrected.

"I can live with that. Thank you." Lance kissed the top of her head like she'd just granted him some marvelous boon. "You're so stiff and your skin is so hot. You're angry with me," he said.

Oh, she so didn't want to have this conversation right now. Or, ever. "This whole conversation is just... can we not do it?"

"Whatever you want, Morgan. Will you tell me one thing, though? What happened that Gwen wants you to fix?"

Morgan looked at him now not with the eyes of a woman watching her lover, but with the eyes of power granted to her by Avalon. He was in pain, obviously. She didn't need to look with any special power to see that. But his aura was tinged with guilt.

Morgan sighed heavily before she spoke. "It's not you, if that's what you're worried about. She's okay that's it over. She said I could have you, actually. Of course, I don't know what I'd do with you. Like you said, it's not like I need a knight in shining armor." Morgan almost choked on her words. "It's Arthur."

Lance looked like he'd been kicked in the balls with his own spurs. "Oh."

Maybe he still had feelings for Gwen after all. It wouldn't be unheard of. He'd spent centuries—Morgan clamped down on that little voice and everything selfish that grasped for him. She was Morgan Le Fey, Evil Enchantress, Seductress, Sorceress, and most importantly, the only title that really mattered—servant of Avalon.

"Maybe you should seek him out. Ask his forgiveness. If Gwen can do it, I'm certain a man such as yourself could ask his oldest friend, the brother of his heart, for forgiveness."

"I don't deserve it." He was suddenly grim, his expression a thundercloud.

"Sometimes, when we want things, we have to ask for them whether we deserve them or not." Morgan did realize that what she said could easily apply to herself, but whereas Lance actually deserved forgiveness, Morgan knew she'd made too many bad choices to ever end up with Happily Ever After.

"You're pretty profound for an Evil Enchantress." His tone was quiet, contemplative.

"Yeah, well, I'd have to be half-stupid not to have learned a little something about human nature after all years meddling in affairs of men."

"You say that like you're not human, Morgan. Don't buy into your own fanfare." He sounded like an oracle handing down a prophecy. And again, that earnest goodness that flared inside of him practically burned her.

"But I'm not. I'm fey, and any part of me that was human died a long time ago when I was consecrated to Avalon. Don't forget, I *am* an Evil Enchantress." Morgan said that as much to remind him as herself. "Gwen is waiting. I have to go."

"Hurry back, witch. Otherwise, I might miss you."

Morgan forced a smile to her face and went outside to meet Gwen without looking back at the white knight who was everything she wanted, but everything she knew she could never have.

"Are you okay?" Gwen asked as soon as she saw her face.

Morgan would have to work on her game face. She couldn't have all of her gushy feelings spread all over face like so much pudding. "Yeah, fine. Lance was worried I was going to drown you, but I assured him you'd survive."

"That was gallant of him. I guess distance does engender a certain fondness."

Morgan cut her eyes to the other women. "What do you mean?"

"Well, just the other day he was telling me he'd like me better if I could learn to talk with my mouth closed. I think if you would've showed up with an offer to drown me, he would've paid you to make it happen."

Morgan couldn't help the tiny giggle that started in the back of her throat like an itch. "I guess the grass is always greener."

"Yeah, have you heard him eat, yet? He sounds like a truffling pig. The day we... ending things..." she paused. "I really considered how hard I'd have to hit him so the popcorn he was chomping on would come out of his nose."

She snorted and the giggle erupted into a fit of full blown laughter.

Yes, the apocalypse was surely nigh when Guinevere du Lac and Morgan Le Fey could be seen wandering down to the resort *together*, their combined laughter sounding much like the honking of demented geese.

# CHAPTER
# NINETEEN

APHRODITE

Yes, Aphrodite decided the world was definitely on its last legs. First, Aeron had turned down sex with her and now, Morgan and Guinevere du Lac were standing at her door.

*Together.*

Morgan didn't stink of any sort of foul curse, but Aphrodite had been fooled before.

She opened the door wide and allowed them to come inside the small, but luxurious hut.

Gwen seemed very nervous. She kept wringing her hands and biting her lip. Aphrodite supposed if she were in the former queen's position—being alone with a witch who hated her and a goddess who happened to be one of said witch's besties, *and* having felt repeatedly wronged by Love —yeah, it would be uncomfortable to say the least.

Aphrodite put on her benign goddess face. "Guinevere du Lac, what is it you wish to ask of Love?"

She looked to Morgan and waited for Morgan to nod

before answering. Well, that was definitely an interesting development—Guinevere looking for Morgan's approval before speaking.

"I was going to say that I'm not asking this for myself, but I suppose I am." She exhaled heavily.

"It's okay to ask for yourself. Did someone tell you it wasn't?"

"Love isn't supposed to be selfish," Guinevere said.

"Sometimes, it is. It's many things. Go on, child."

"I heard that to stop his pain, you took Hades heart."

"I did." Aphrodite studied her for a moment. "Are you asking me to take your heart?"

Gwen closed her eyes and a tear slipped down her cheek. Aphrodite could see now why two great men had ruined themselves for her. She was beautiful, delicate, and oh-so enchanting even in her grief. If Aphrodite wasn't just as beautiful and enchanting, she might be a bit jealous. "In a sense, I suppose I am. I'm asking you to make it so that Arthur doesn't remember loving me."

Aphrodite was curious to know more about Gwen's motivations, or better yet, what Gwen believed her motivations to be. Aphrodite knew that her request was born of the deepest and truest love. "An interesting request. Why not ask me to make it so he never loved you?"

"That's where I'm being selfish. Those memories are for me. I want to remember what it was like when he did love me."

"And punish yourself?" Aphrodite asked.

"It is bittersweet, but I'll take the bitter if I can still have the sweet."

Aphrodite could see that she answered honestly and her intentions were not only pure, but rooted in love.

"Why do think Arthur would choose any differently?

He's King of Avalon, he knows I'm on the island and he hasn't sought me out."

"Because he can't imagine not loving me. He's always loved me. But now, I see it's bringing him more pain than anything. I just want to save him. He deserves better."

"Better than you, or better than his pain?" Aphrodite asked kindly.

"Both," Guinevere confessed in a quiet voice.

Aphrodite sighed. She reached out and measured their threads of Love and Fate. They were all tangled up and knotted in on each other. What a mess. She saw Morgan's looped and tied with a little bow amongst the skein, and Aphrodite almost laughed out loud.

"Guinevere, I find your request to be made of a pure heart, but I will not take that from him he wishes to keep. You must tell him what you've asked of me and if he comes to me of his own volition, I will do as you've asked."

"Thank you, Aphrodite."

"Thank you, Guinevere, for not blaming me."

Guinevere cocked her head to the side. "Why ever would I blame you?"

"When love goes wrong, I'm always at fault. Or so most mortals think."

"I'm not mortal, anymore. And I screwed everything up all on my own. Lance was a dream that was better left to the unrequited fantasy of a heart that hadn't been tested. Both of them were ideals and I broke them. Not love. But me. If my love had been true, I wouldn't have ruined them so I could have what I wanted."

"Oh honey." Aphrodite hugged her. "You made some mistakes. We all do. They did, too. You went from one side of the spectrum, to believing you'd done no wrong to believing you've done *all* the wrong. It's time to stop in the middle."

"I just want to fix this." Her face was crumpled with regret.

"Some things can only be fixed with time." Aphrodite thought about her own situation. "A lot of time."

"Thank you," Guinevere said. Then she looked at Morgan. "I already got one hug out of you, I'm not going to push it."

"Better not. Hugging Morgan Le Fey is like making out with a thistle. You're lucky you didn't get some thorns." Aphrodite grinned.

"Yeah, and uh, you know, don't tell anyone about that part. I don't want it getting out," Morgan grumped.

"I swear, I won't." Guinevere moved toward the door. "Looks like I have to face the dragon one more time. Thank you, again."

When she was gone, Morgan turned to her. "So, spill."

Aphrodite was wide-eyed. "What do you mean?"

"You know exactly what I mean. I know Ares has been on the island. I can feel him. And you don't have the look of a woman recently laid like tile. Aeron has been here, but *not here*, if you get my drift."

"The drift has definitely made its point." Aphrodite huffed, and all trace of the benevolent all-knowing goddess was gone. In its place was a very frustrated woman. "Ares won't take the hint. I looked, Morgan." She sighed heavily and flopped back on the large bed.

"You *look* looked?"

Aphrodite nodded miserably. "Yeah. He's supposed to end up with Morrigan. Do you know her?"

"Not really. Never made the effort. I used to get her mail and she'd get mine. We were confused for a lot of mythology. But she seems like a meaner version of me, if that's possible."

"She's like me and you, if we made one awesome goddess. Being both hearth and war, she's perfect for Ares." Aphrodite exhaled heavily.

"Are you okay?" Morgan asked, concern tinging her voice.

"I guess. I mean, I'm the Goddess of Love, with the capital letters. So that means when Love works out like it's supposed to, it increases my power. It makes something click inside me that's a bliss unlike anything else. But it's *Ares*. I always thought we were forever and we're not. All those years, wasted. There's no part of my history that he hasn't been there for. When we were godlings, he'd tie knots in my braids and I'd make him fall in love with his swords."

Morgan smiled. "And you'll always have that. Even if he warmongers off with Morrigan."

"I know. I can't even say I don't like it, I guess I don't know how to feel."

"I know what you mean."

"I'm sure you do. How's the hookup with Lance coming along? Must be interesting if you were bringing Guinevere to see me."

"I can't even talk about it. It's a great big bag of crap and honestly, I just want to put a tie on it and put it in the corner."

"So, we have to smell it, but you don't want to think about it?" If it was crap, the best thing to do was dump it like kitty litter.

"Pretty much. Just for now."

"Do you want me to look?" Aphrodite was dying to know what happened. She was sure that Lance loved her friend. He'd always had a thing for Morgan. He'd always been pissed he had a thing for her, but it had been there nonetheless.

"What do you mean? Look to see if he loves me? Goddess, no. Not in a million years. And no, I don't want you to make him love me, either." Morgan eyed her like she would a child who'd gotten caught with her hand in the cookie jar.

Aphrodite liked that about her. Morgan had never been intimidated by her. In fact, Aphrodite doubted Morgan would be intimidated by Zeus himself standing hip to hip with the Cronus *and* the Kraken.

"Why not? I can help you, so let me. I swear, you're the only person in any dimension who hasn't taken advantage of being my friend." Aphrodite really wanted to do this for Morgan.

"And I never will." Morgan replied gently.

"But...but I want you to."

"Get over it." Her friend grinned. "I really don't want to know. Right now, I can still hope."

"What if I told you that Lance would love you?"

"Then I'd find a way to screw it up. I really don't want to know. Really." Morgan said emphatically. "Plus, I'm not going to let you use this thing with me to hide from your own issues."

Aphrodite sagged. "Damn it, why not?"

"Well, what about a compromise?" A mischievous grin curved Morgan's mouth.

"You look like you're about to suggest some real trouble. I'm in." Aphrodite mirrored her expression. She was better at meddling in other people's love lives than handling her own anyway. Not that she'd ever admit it out loud. After all, who wanted to deal with a Goddess of Love who didn't know her ass from a gopher hole? Not her, that was for sure.

Morgan laughed and she sounded very much like the wicked witch she claimed to be. "Good. Since my relationships are out and you don't want to talk about yours, how about we stir the pot in Mordred's? He needs it."

"Oh!" Aphrodite gasped. "I've been so busy I forgot to update you on what happened to him. The curse that pissed me off when I got here? I'm sure Artemis told you, it was Vivienne."

Morgan raised a brow. "Oh really?"

"Yes. And she didn't just piss me off. She pissed Mordred off too."

"What did she do to my son?" Suddenly, Morgan was all avenging lioness of doom. "He's paid Vivienne's price more times than any one person should ever have to."

Aphrodite gave a delicate shrug. "He might have earned it this time."

Morgan's eyes narrowed. Aphrodite had never seen one woman express so much with just a subtle shift of her eyes. She definitely had the bearing of a goddess.

"Oh really?"

"He pretended to be Arthur and played at seducing her until she surrendered. *Then* he revealed himself."

"She had it coming. But I think, maybe, he might have earned it, too. What did she do and can I fix it?"

"She cursed him to fall in love with the next woman he kissed."

"Which I'm really hoping was Artemis."

"Actually, it was. Convenient, yes?" Aphrodite grinned. "And I cursed Vivienne for what she did."

"Can you maybe not? She's the Lady of the Lake, Keeper of Avalon. We kind of need her magick."

"Oh no. She's lost her magick. You are the new Lady of the Lake. In fact, the power should hit you any minute."

Morgan closed her eyes. "I... fuck."

"What's the problem?"

"The problem is that Vivienne is Lance's *mother*. So basically, she lost her job and it's my fault. Great."

"Uh, how is it your fault?"

"Because... just because." Morgan couldn't articulate exactly why it was her fault, but Aphrodite could see where she was coming from and how Lance would think that. But damn it all anyway, Vivienne wasn't a goddess and she shouldn't be trespassing on goddess territory. The world was bigger than Avalon and Aphrodite was bound and determined to teach her that lesson.

"I was just giving Artemis the I'm Going To Be Your Mother-In-Law talk and here I go and screw it up with Vivienne."

"I will smite her so hard if she blames you. She did this to herself, Morgan. To. Her. Self. You've served her and Avalon faithfully for almost all of your life. I really don't think she's going to blame you. And you should have heard the curses she hurled at Guinevere when Lance brought her home instead of you. She'd planned for you to end up together. I know she loves her son and you. If she didn't, the curse I hit her with would've been much nastier, I promise you."

Morgan sighed. "Looks like even meddling in other people's affairs, our own crap still finds the light of day."

"Let's get back to Mordred. If he asks me to lift the curse, what do you want me to do?"

"It would just figure that he had to antagonize the one woman whose magick could really screw up his day." Morgan shook her head. "But he was always like that. I'm sure by now he's figured out that I threw Artemis at him. How does she feel about all of this?"

"I don't think she knows. She definitely doesn't want to fall for him just because he's first. I can see that in yellow highlighter all over her aura."

"As much as I love my son, it might do him good to have his heart broken. It's never happened before."

"Most mothers wish for their children to never experience heartache. Why would you wish that on him?"

"So he knows what it feels like to be on the other end of his schemes. As I said, I love my son, but he's been a weapon his whole life. It's time he learned how to live. Pain is sometimes a part of that. I wish it wasn't, because he's had enough suffering. Just not the kind that teaches the good lessons."

Aphrodite smiled. "You know, I think it's past time that you became Lady of the Lake. Vivienne hasn't been willing or able to teach her followers these things for a long time."

"I don't want it, Aphrodite. I really don't."

"Which is why it's yours. That's how these things work."

"Well, we're magickal beings. We can un-work them."

"Un-work? Is that even a thing?"

"It could be," Morgan insisted.

"Fine. Want to help me figure out how to tame a dragon?"

"Is that a euphemism?" Morgan grinned.

"Actually, yes. And no. Ares and I are over and things are going well for Artemis, so I decided maybe Aeron might be a nice distraction."

"What's the problem?"

"His dragon."

Morgan snort-giggled. "You're kidding me, right?"

"No. He fed me some line about how his dragon wants me and—"

"*His dragon*. Goddess, that's as bad as love gun."

Aphrodite realized this was payback for her conversation with Artemis on her birthday. Love gun. Swinging Dick Stick of Doom. Purple-headed womb ferret... "At least he didn't say his anaconda."

"Yes, thank you, Sir Mix A Lot."

They giggled. "But really, what's a goddess to do to get a little tail?"

"The answer is rather simple." Morgan smiled at her. "To tame the dragon, you should become one. Literally."

# TWENTY

VIVIENNE

For Vivienne, it was as if her very soul had been torn from her body.

And maybe it had been.

For so long, Avalon had been part of her. She'd tried to live her office, to be nothing more than Lady of the Lake because in her heart, she'd been so much less.

She didn't know if she was being punished or rewarded.

"Vivienne? What happened?" Hector asked, his palm cupped her cheek.

"I—I'm no longer Lady of the Lake. My magick is gone." She held up her hands and looked at them as if they didn't belong to her. Yes, she'd thought that the mantle was too much to bear and so it had been taken from her.

But without it, what was she?

*Who* was she?

She looked to Hector, as if he somehow had the answer. "Without Avalon, who am I?"

"You are not without Avalon. You're still here. You still walk upon the green summer grasses, you still breathe the sweet air, and if you go outside, you'll still look up at the same sky. Avalon is in your blood as much as you are within her shores. Magick or no."

Suddenly, her little cottage was cloying, suffocating. It was as if she had to run outside to see if she did indeed breathe the same air, could feel the grasses under her toes and look upon the perpetually blue sky.

Vivienne ran outside and the warm sun cascading warm and gentle over her face. She inhaled deeply, smelling apples and grass, and a newness she couldn't name. Looking up into the sky, she did see the oceans of infinite blue above her.

All was the same.

Yet, everything was different.

Hector emerged behind her, silent and strong. Always the protector—even now.

"I remember when the priestesses came for me. I was terrified and hopeful all at once." Vivienne bit her lip, but that didn't stop the tide of memory that washed over her.

"How old were you?" he asked, inviting her to continue her tale.

"I was ten when they took me as a novice. Back in those days, the Priestesses of Avalon had more sway than any king or lord. If they'd said for the sake of the people I was to go, then I would go." Vivienne sighed. "But I can't say I didn't want it. As soon as I was old enough to know of Avalon, or the powerful, educated women who basked in the light of Avalon, I wanted to be one. I looked around my village, at the lives of my mother, my sisters, and I never wanted that. They were all old before their time, pushing one squalling child after another into a world of violence, darkness, and strife. I was so sure that if I could just be a priestess, I could change all of it."

"And you did, Vivienne." His expression was tender.

"How did I do that? I brought down an empire. I ruined my son's life. I—"

Hector interrupted her. "You of all people know that there is always free will. You may have set the stage, you may have even provided some direction, but always, the choice lies with those who acted. Not you. Morgan chose to seduce Arthur and bear his child. Arthur chose to be seduced. Lance fell in love with Gwen, and she with him. They both chose what happened next. You did not choose for them. Stop owning their blame."

"At least if I own their blame, I can do something useful."

"You said yourself Camelot was a dream and it was something golden and pure for man to aspire to. It wasn't meant to last. And yet, when you look in the world, can you not see your influence? Arthur's story inspires so many to do more, to be more. You would change that?"

"I don't know," Vivienne confessed. "What if Camelot hadn't fallen?"

"Nothing lasts forever, Vivienne. Everything that is born must die."

"Why? We're here. We were born and living on Avalon, we will never die."

"Change comes to all things, even Avalon." He took her hand. "Come, let me show you."

An unreasonable terror knifed through her. She pulled away. "No. I can't."

He grabbed her, his strong arms trapping her against him. "Why not?"

Her mind clouded as her brain could only focus on the

hot steel of his hand on her back, the stone wall of his chest, and the fire that flared between them.

"Let me go." She struggled against him.

"No, Vivienne."

"You wouldn't have dared this if I still had my magick," she said in a low tone, fighting panic.

"You didn't need this from me when you still had your magick."

"I don't want you." She shoved uselessly at his biceps.

He laughed, but it wasn't the warm sound that sent shivers up and down her spine. It was cold and mirthless. Then he whispered against her ear, "You made that plainly obvious when you called out for Arthur instead of me when it was me between your thighs. I've already told you, I've accepted my penance. Perhaps this is yours. But instead of accepting it, you're hiding from it. I never knew you to be a coward, Vivienne."

"I told you that you didn't know me at all," she whispered. *He was right*. She was a coward. She always had been. Deep down underneath all of her bluster, she was afraid of everything. Vivienne didn't need him to say it for her to know that it was true.

He released her, disgust twisting his handsome features. "Maybe I don't. But you may take cold comfort in this, my lady. If you don't have the strength of character to meet change, you aren't strong enough to engineer anyone's fate. Least of all the shining beacon that was Camelot. Let your conscious be clear of that."

Hector said this last as if he were spitting out something foul. And it cut her somehow. He'd never spoken a harsh word to her, never displayed any emotion when he was around her except service, loyalty and devotion. In short, she was an ass. She shouldn't have said those things, shouldn't have said that she didn't want him because it wasn't true. She was only trying to hurt him, she'd lashed out like a dog backed into a corner. And that was ridiculous. He'd only been trying to reassure her, to show her things that he thought would comfort her. Instead, they'd scared her even more.

"Hector, I—"

He held up his hand to stay her. "No. You spoke the words you meant to speak. And I did the same. There is no apology needed for truth."

"Who said I was going to apologize?" Vivienne said defiantly. In that moment, he was every inch the dazzling knight, right down to that cocky tilt to his chin.

"The set to your shoulders. The frown on your lips." He watched her intently for a moment. "The soft pity in your eyes."

"Maybe the pity was for myself."

"Most assuredly." He nodded. "We're both wretched creatures this day."

"You were right. I am afraid. I'm terrified."

"I know." His voice was soft again. "And perhaps I pushed too hard. You've just lost your magick. I imagine it's like your sword and armor. I would be lost and I admit, even afraid, without my own."

Goddess, he was just too perfect. Even in his flaws, he was an ideal.

Her words were a dagger that had stuck home. She knew she'd hurt him, and it was her aim to hurt him so he'd stop, but she should've known that even if she hurt him, she'd never sway him from what he thought was his duty. Now, they'd been spoken and she couldn't take them back.

He already believed he wasn't good enough, and that was her doing as well. She had to try to fix this. "I was only trying to hurt you. I was afraid." She looked down at her hands, unable to face him. "I still am."

"Your words will not make me leave you. I vowed myself to you again after your magick was gone. I am, and will always be, your champion. Lady of the Lake, or not." He reached out slowly and lifted her chin so she looked into his eyes. "Lover or not."

"Hector," she began, but she was at an utter loss. Vivienne knew that was the truth of it, but she also know that she didn't deserve his loyalty, or his devotion.

Instead of saying anything else, she turned her face into the palm of his hand. Goddess, but his hands were a thing of wonder. So strong, but so gentle. He touched her as if she were a butterfly he knew he could crush.

And he could.

Now that she was without her magick, she was defenseless against him, or anyone else who sought to do her harm.

*Mordred.*

The spell she'd cast on him had been broken. Oh, when he discovered Vivienne was powerless—fear reared again, a King Cobra whose fangs dripped with venom. Mordred was what she'd made of him, a weapon who'd been wrought only for destruction.

"You tremble, Vivienne."

She swallowed hard, her fingers curled around his wrist.

"Surely you don't fear me as well."

"Never. I fear how I've hurt you, I fear how I've failed you. But I don't fear you."

"You needn't fear anyone, Vivienne. I won't let anyone or anything hurt you."

The caress melted into an embrace and Vivienne went into his arms easily. It was safe there, within the circle of his arms. Nothing bad could touch her and all the things she feared faded away with the steady beat of his heart.

He smelled so good and being pressed so intimately against him, it conjured all sorts of scenarios. If he'd take her now in the sweet grass... but Vivienne realized she was still only thinking of herself. Of her own needs.

Hector had wanted to show her something. She had to let him. No matter that she was afraid.

Vivienne was hit with another revelation.

By being afraid, trapped in her fear, she was doing him the gravest insult. She was telling him again that he wasn't worthy. That he wasn't enough. She was telling him that she didn't trust him to keep his word—to keep her safe.

Shame was a sour putrid bile in her throat.

"Hector, you said you had something you wanted to show me. I'm sorry I was afraid, that I didn't trust in you. Will you show me now?"

"Vivienne, if you are not ready to see, I can't show you."

Well, that was a ball of mystery wrapped in an enigma frosted with a riddle. Now she knew how other people felt when they were talking to her. It wasn't pleasant.

"I am ready." She took a deep breath. "I trust you." And she did trust him.

"It's not only me that you must trust in, but magick that is not yours."

"Whose?" Something sharp twisted in her gut.

Hector smiled. "You said you trust me. If I trust in it, shouldn't that be enough?"

Again, he was right. Goddess, but how she hated learning lessons. They were always uncomfortable.

"Okay," she squeaked. Irritation at herself bubbled. She was Vivienne du Lac. She did not squeak like some timid mouse. Even if that's what she felt on the inside. "Yes," she clarified.

"Then let's go." He pulled a large amethyst from a pouch at his waist and a purple smoke surrounded them.

This was how he and Lance had gotten off the island without her knowledge or her magick, she realized. It could only belong to Morgan or Mordred. Probably Mordred, because Morgan would've told her and her son never would've asked Morgan for a damn thing.

She clung tightly to Hector and when she could see nothing but fog, for a moment, she feared drowning in the ether. Vivienne forced herself to breathe slowly, to think about only Hector's arms around her, the steady, sure beat of his heart. He was not afraid. She would not be afraid.

Even when it felt as if her skin and bones had turned to purple dust and she was nothing air.

"We're flying Vivienne, look."

She didn't want to look, but there was something about his voice. It was light, free, and joyous. So she opened her eyes.

Avalon was a tiny, verdant dot in a light blue waters, surrounded by an impenetrable wall of fog. Thankfully, it wasn't purple.

This was the first time she'd been off Avalon since they'd gone into the mist. She'd watched the world outside through her crystal ball, and she'd kept up with modern advances. But she'd thought it was her duty to stay there, on the island.

It hit her that she'd been hiding. Not just from her mistakes, but from living.

Oh Goddess, how did she fix this?

She clung tighter to Hector and realized that maybe she wasn't an island herself after all. Maybe she did need someone, and maybe that was okay.

Just maybe.

CHAPTER

# TWENTY-ONE

ARTEMIS

He still hadn't punched her V-Card.

His tongue probably had a callus on it. Maybe even a blister. He'd even sprained his wrist bringing her off. He'd done every delightful, delectable thing to her that she could begin to imagine. Some things she couldn't.

But still, he hadn't taken her virginity.

They were sitting outside on the chaise lounges nibbling on cheese, fruit and chocolate to recover their strength. He'd even procured pomegranate truffles so she wouldn't be homesick.

He saw to her every need.

Except that one.

Artemis couldn't help but wonder if she'd done something wrong.

175

*Tell him to feed you a truffle.* Aphrodite's voice resonated in her head.

Hmm. She wasn't sure how she felt about that. Was she listening in while they'd been—

*No. Just do it. Goddess of Love out.*

Artemis smiled and turned her head to look at him. By Zeus, but he was beautiful. The contours of muscle, the smooth perfection of his skin. She wanted to touch him all over, pet him like she would the Golden Fleece.

"I think I need another truffle." She licked her lips.

Mordred focused on her, the intensity in his amethyst eyes setting her body on fire yet again. "That wouldn't be a ploy to get me to bring you one, would it?" he teased.

"No. Of course not." Her gaze strayed to his hands and memories of what those talented fingers had done to her washed over her. She shivered delicately. "It's a ploy to get you to bring it and feed it to me."

"Really?" The corner of his mouth curled up in a smirk and he proceeded to fulfill her desire.

He brought her one of the succulent treats and offered it to her between two fingers.

Now what was she supposed to do? Probably something that had to do with sucking on his fingers and miming a blow job. The idea had merit. She'd like to have him at her mercy the same way she was at his.

She opened her mouth delicately, she didn't want to look like a seal begging for a fish.

He pushed his fingers to her lips slowly, his eyes focused on hers.

Artemis knew truffles could give orgasms, but she had a feeling that this would be ten times as intense. Her tongue darted out to taste the truffle, and brushed the sides of his fingers.

They were salty, and she tasted herself. So it was kind of sweet too.

And he knew it.

Well, of course he knew it.

But the expression on his face, it was pure lust. Need. Desire.

So she did it again.

"I would tell you that you play with fire, lovely goddess, but I think you want to burn in it."

His voice was both sin and redemption as the decadent chocolate melted on her tongue.

Artemis wanted to lay back and let him do every naughty thing to her three times over again, but what she wanted more was for him to experience that kind of ecstasy. She wondered if anyone had ever pleased him just for the sake of his pleasure. Not hoping to get something in return, either a favor, a seduction, or making him love them.

Yes, the denizens of Olympus were good at all of the above, but pleasure for the sake of pleasure was practically a mantra.

She grew bolder, sliding her tongue up the inside of his finger and closing her slender hand around his wrist to anchor him there. Artemis was a hunter, so viewing his pleasure like prey made her a master. She sought it out, stalked it, honed in on its weakness and then went in for the kill.

Artemis sucked his finger deep into the hot, wet cavern of her mouth and swirled her tongue around the digit, the taste of the truffle completely forgotten.

She released his wrist and tugged on the waistband of his jeans. When they didn't do as she wished, she used her magick to make them disintegrate.

His cock was hard, and thick, purposeful, just like a sword. She found it beautiful. Artemis touched her tongue to the head, just like she'd done with his fingers and then took him into her mouth. She dug her nails into his hips, marking half-moons in his perfect skin.

That was her stamp. Her mark.

*Hers.*

He growled low in his throat as she serviced him, his fingers tangling in her hair, his back arching.

But if she brought him to completion now, it would be over, and he'd said he liked games. This had to be more than pleasure for his body, it had to be for his mind, too. She disappeared and manifested next to the edge of the copse of trees several feet away.

The look on his face was fantastic. It was incredulous, it was bereft, but it was also predatory. He was already plotting how to capture her and since the hunt was her domain, she knew intrinsically that he loved every minute of it.

She took off her bikini top and threw it at him. "Take me if you can, Le Fey."

Artemis darted into the trees. She loved the thrill of the chase, and even now, she was only pretending to be the hunted. She was still closing in on his pleasure.

He moved stealthily through the underbrush behind her, he was fast, but he was smart. That made her tingle and bite her lip, too.

Artemis camouflaged herself by merging into a tree. Its presence was warm and welcoming, and it wholly approved of the ruse.

He paused, just steps from her. "I know you're here. You smell like pomegranates and chocolate."

Mordred took his time, inspecting each branch and

stone. "You're a naughty goddess to make me run through the forest naked."

Very naked.

He was every inch the Horned God.

She giggled. She couldn't help herself.

Mordred reached into the tree and yanked her out.

"That was easy." He wore a smug look.

As much as she wanted to be caught, it was over much too soon and he was too proud of himself. "Was it?" She smiled and snapped her fingers. A rope tied around his ankle and hoisted him up into the canopy.

His horned godhood flapping as he went.

"I will get you," he vowed, and his voice almost sounded dangerous.

"I certainly hope so." Artemis laughed and fled again.

Part of her wanted to wait for him because she did indeed want to be caught. But another part of her said that if he couldn't catch her fair and square, he didn't deserve the spoils of the hunt.

She smacked her inner goddess down. It was that bitch's fault she hadn't experienced all of these earthly delights yet. She could just be quiet.

Artemis crept back toward the clearing hating herself with every step. She looked up and saw him hanging there —noticeably deflated—and miserable. Her shoulders slumped.

Strong arms closed around her and Artemis was suddenly done playing. She fought for all she was worth. How dare this unknown mortal touch her and--

"Artemis!"

The cloud of fury dissipated and she turned in the embrace and realized it was Mordred who held her. He'd laid a trap for her.

"Oh, you sneaky bastard." The admiration was back. He knew she wouldn't leave him hanging, even though she should have.

"I win."

"Wrong again." She melted out of his arms into a stream and rather than being irritated with her, he laughed.

It was a musical sound, like a dark aria. She wanted to wrap herself in it.

"Just wait until I catch you, gorgeous."

That's exactly what she was counting on.

She took goddess form in a clearing not too far from the trap, but found his arms around her again. It was as if he'd traveled in the stream with her.

Instead of saying anything sarcastic, this time, he just kissed her.

And that made it okay for him to win.

Artemis surrendered to his arms, his kiss, the moment.

It was absolutely perfect.

Until a sudden cough startled her. She would've broken away and investigated, but Mordred didn't seem to care there was someone in the clearing with them. She could almost hear his thinking.

*If they're looking, they deserve what they get.*

But that subtle clearing of a throat sounded a lot like Apollo. Her brother. And her skin was suddenly very, very warm.

"Oh, for fuck's sake." he grumbled, but he didn't release her.

Yep, in all his sunshine-out-his-ass glory. Her brother. In the flesh.

"Artemis, are you okay?" he asked, round balls of fire like solar flares gathered at his fists.

"I'm actually a little busy."

"But, but..." Apollo stuttered. "You're the eternal virgin." He said this as if it was something she didn't know.

"I'm done with that. Time for new things."

"Put on a toga, for Zeus's sake." He sounded incredibly scandalized.

She and Mordred were suddenly both wearing togas that her brother had manifested. His was black. She had to say it made him look even more like a villain and she liked it.

"For Zeus's sake or for your sake?" Artemis asked.

Apollo shrugged. "Whatever you're more comfortable with." He eyed Mordred disdainfully. "Who is this wretched creature?"

Artemis narrowed her eyes. "I would think for someone who is married to the Goddess of Night, you'd understand my attraction to the dark."

She waited for Mordred to say something snarky, inappropriate and completely disrespectful. Apollo would choke on his own spit. And Artemis kind of liked it that way. For centuries, he'd been the one living La Vida Olympus and it was time Artemis had some fun of her own. He was as bad about turning her swains into something unpleasant as she was. In fact, it was her brother who'd educated her on the evils of males and then after one of her supplicants had tried to attack her, she'd been content to follow Apollo's directives.

Mordred surprised her again. Instead of flipping her brother the proverbial bird, he reached out to shake her brother's hand. No one had ever done that before. No one treated Apollo like a mortal—not that he was overly pompous about it. All gods were a bit pompous to one extreme or another, but... it was just too weird.

Apollo flared like glow stick, his flesh would be scalding

to the touch, but Mordred didn't flinch. He didn't pull away. He simply shook the god's hand while his flesh smoked.

Artemis cried out. "Stop that! I need that hand. It's magickal."

Apollo went dark. It was like turning off a light. "You *what?*"

"He's not hurting me. I'm here of my own free will, Apollo. On some level, you know that or you would've already turned him to ash."

Apollo eyed him again. "I don't like it."

She appreciated that her brother was trying to look out for her, but really, this was too much. "But I do." She said softly.

He still didn't look at Artemis, but he frowned. "If you hurt my sister, I swear to Tartarus I'll—"

"Yeah, yeah. You'll roast my face off. I get it." He grinned as his hand healed. "If she were my sister…" He looked at Artemis. "Who am I kidding? If she were my sister I'd still think she was hot."

"Don't be gross." Artemis teased.

"What? It's the truth and I'm a bad boy, remember?"

Apollo shifted uncomfortably. "Hey, I'm still here."

"So don't be." Artemis hoped he'd take the hint.

"What's your name?" he ignored her.

"Mordred Le Fey, bastard extraordinaire and Avalon tourist attraction at your service."

Apollo raised a brow as if he planned on more interrogation.

"I appreciate the meet and greet, but we were in the middle of something. So if we could take this up later?" Mordred eyed him. "Look, I can't hurt her. It's physically impossible. Nothing is going to happen to her that she's not into, okay?"

"Oh, and how can I believe that? I've heard about you, Le Fey. You did a number on Medusa."

"And Circe," he agreed easily. "But I've been cursed to fall in love with Artemis. So if anything, my mother should be questioning Artemis as to her intentions instead of this meeting of the manwhores."

Apollo glared at him and his skin pinkened to a burn. "Former manwhore. As you'd better be."

"Can you guys please, *please* stop with the whole clashing of antlers, here? Apollo, you're not the Great Stag or the Horned One."

"I'm the horny one." Apollo and Mordred quipped at the same time.

They turned to look at each other, sharing a knowing glance and laughed.

But Artemis was fed up. "Maybe you two should shag each other."

She stomped off, but didn't get far.

"That wasn't as ugly as I thought it would be." Mordred wrapped his arms around her waist.

"What?"

"Meeting your brother."

"Why would you assume you'd meet him? He's been too busy with Ephie and his new wife to ruin any of my plans." She was still irritated.

"Artemis, come on. You're going to fall in love with me. If we're going to be together forever, I imagine at some point, I'd have to meet your family. Unless you plan on keeping me in a cave somewhere, strapped down for your pleasure. Which, I could be into."

She broke away from him.

"Look, you're hot and everything, but I don't want to be in love," Artemis said.

183

"Me either. But that's not up to us."

"I said I'd have Aphrodite break your curse, so really, this is just dumb."

"What if I don't want her to break it," he whispered.

Artemis actually gulped. It was an audible sound, completely exaggerated. But it still didn't sum up how she felt about that statement.

"I signed up for sex, not love."

"I see. You just want to ride the ride, get your souvenir and go home." His voice was devoid of any emotion.

The way he said it broke her heart just a little bit. She wanted to recapture what they'd felt before her stupid brother had interrupted them. The high of the chase, the take down, the excitement in their veins.

She'd been afraid of sex, but she was even more terrified of love. She'd seen how bad it could be, the things that happened to people who fell in love. If Aphrodite could see her train of thought, she'd kill her.

But love was for other people. Not for her. Not romantic love, anyway.

And to be loved by a man such as Mordred Le Fey? No, Artemis wasn't that lucky. The curse would fade in its own time and when it did, where would she be?

"You don't understand."

"Explain it to me." Still no emotion.

She looked up into his eyes and those beautiful pools were flat. Like they'd been replaced with paste jewels instead of the real thing.

"Curses break. Curses fade. And those that meddle in love—"

"You mean like what my mother did to Sir Bitchalot and his lady fair? She's still paying for it."

"As will Vivienne. The magick they wrought will turn to

dust and whatever was built on top of it will crumble. Can't you see that?"

"All I know is that curse or not, this is something I've never experienced before. It's warm, Artemis. I've never been warm."

"I'd say you were plenty warm when my brother was trying to light you on fire." She tried to make light.

"That's nothing compared to what burns in me. My whole life, I've been cold. Empty. My mother wasn't unkind, and she loves me in her way. But I've never forgotten why I was born. Or what I was for. But I do with you."

His confession crushed her. She didn't speak.

He laughed, and while it was mirthless, it wasn't cold. "You don't feel the same, do you? Even after everything that happened between us. This is a first for me." He nodded slowly. "It would figure the woman I love after all these years doesn't love me back. I suppose it's what I deserve."

No, he didn't deserve that at all. Artemis didn't know how to tell him that without digging the hole deeper, so instead, she kissed him.

His lips were hard and unyielding under her gentle assault, but in moments, he was kissing her back, his hands roving her body and tearing at her toga.

He lay her down in the grass and took everything she offered.

# CHAPTER
# TWENTY-TWO

GWEN

L ike any of the other times she'd had to speak to Arthur, Gwen debated not going. It took her a day to work up the courage. It was always a trial to face him.

In fact, she'd rather go back and face her accusers in Camelot a hundred times over than face Arthur and his goodness, his pain, and his enduring love for her.

It was even worse for her now that she accepted her actions were wrong. She had betrayed him. No matter what he'd done, or perceived wrongs, Gwen had made the choice to break her vows.

Facing him was her penance, and she could accept that. What she couldn't accept was that he had to suffer for her mistakes.

He'd endured enough.

So with that, she found herself standing in front of the door to his castle with Aphrodite's offer in hand.

He opened the door slowly. "I wondered if you were going to knock or stand there all day."

His breath stank of good whiskey and there was the smell of another woman's perfume on him.

She couldn't be angry and she no longer had the right to be hurt. But she kept remembering his lips on hers, the way he told her he'd be anything for her, and then the pain in his eyes before he walked away.

This visit wasn't about her anyway. It was about him.

"Can we talk, or do you have company?"

"Maybe we could talk *with* my company," he drawled, and Gwen was under the distinct impression he'd just propositioned her for something crude.

She couldn't stop now and if a proposition was the least of his insults, well, she could live with that. Gwen might even take him up on it next time he offered. Maybe that would knock her off the stupid pedestal he still had her on. She didn't how or why he still thought so well of her, but she didn't deserve it.

And neither did he. "This isn't about them. This is about you."

"Not you and me?" Arthur asked as if he were asking about the weather rather than something that had ripped his heart in half.

She shook her head no.

He swung the door wide and what she saw both fascinated and horrified her. It was fitting, she supposed, that Greeks were on the island. Even the gods had never seen debauchery like this. Even having been a married woman and living the long years she had, she blushed. It was almost as if Dionysus himself was on the island. She looked around for that jolly bastard. There were couples in every state of embrace and *dishabille*, sometimes more than a couple. Hell, who was she kidding? This was an all out orgy. All of the God of Plenty's parties were like this one.

As usual, it was as if Arthur knew her thoughts. "No, Dionysus is not here. But he sent wine." He motioned to a couple of casks on the table.

Suddenly all her bravado was gone. She was curious, she'd always wanted to know and sometimes, she'd had fantasies about taking part. In the dirtier ones, she got to have both Arthur and Lance. And when Lance really pissed her off, Arthur put Excalibur in a not so nice place.

"I can come back later." But Gwen knew she'd never muster the courage, coward that she was. There was a part of her that wanted him to tell her to leave and then she'd be free of this. She could put it out of her head. She didn't have to think about him doing these things, being part of all this hedonism.

After all, even if she told him Aphrodite could take his pain, what about his pleasure?

This was what his life had been for these many long years. He was a fucking tourist attraction. He chose to live this way. That wouldn't change just because Aphrodite took his pain away. He wouldn't do these things unless he liked them.

But then he did exactly what the rest of her wanted him to. "Oh, no. You're here now. Come in, Gwen. Come see what it's like to be me."

"Spare me. You chose this," she snarled. How dare he try to play on her guilt? Her prostrations sounded weak even in her own head.

But he turned on her like an abused animal turns on its tormentor. "Spare you? *You?*" He pushed her against the wall and their mouths collided. He obviously meant to punish her, but his kisses were never a penance. He broke the kiss, his breathing heavy and ragged. "Always you, Gwen. It's always about you."

And it was. Whether she made it about herself, or he did. It was always about her. His pain. His suffering. Even his pleasure. He did these things because of his her.

"I'm sorry."

"I am utterly sick of sorry," he hissed against her mouth. "I'm sick of being sorry I can't be everything you want." His fingers tightened around her arms. "And I'm sick of hearing you say that *you're* sorry. From the first time you turned me out of our marriage bed, to when you confessed your infidelity, to when you broke me. And all I got was sorry. *Fuck your sorry, Guinevere.*"

As odd as it was, his rage soothed her. She'd been waiting for it for so long. This was what she understood, this she could process, and this could atone for.

"No, don't fuck sorry. Fuck me, instead."

This time she was the aggressor and she knew all the power was hers. She didn't need to be stronger than he was, she didn't need to slam him against the wall the way he'd done to her. All she had to do was rise up on her tiptoes, her lips like butterfly wings brushing against his.

That was it. Because in a way, it broke him. That softness was a hammer that shattered him. Gwen knew that, but she didn't wield her weapon without mercy.

Who would've thought she could go from angsting about the size of her ass in her yoga pants to this confident, powerful creature?

Maybe that's what she'd been looking for in Lance. To feel beautiful, to feel powerful. Arthur told her she was beautiful, but he never made her feel like she was anything more than the spoils of war. Something to be kept in the treasure room. She'd never known how much he loved her.

She'd been too worried about herself to let him love her. But now it was so obvious in the way he kissed her, his hands gentle even after his display of violence.

He yanked her hard against him as if to punish her for daring to touch his pain. And she liked it. This wasn't Arthur the Statesman, the politician, or even the tourist attraction.

This was Arthur the Warlord—Arthur, the Once and Future King.

Gwen melted into him, but she wasn't without her own fire. She clawed at his shoulders, her tongue dueling for dominance against his. He moaned into her mouth, evidence of his arousal hard against her belly.

"Does Her Highness really want to be fucked against the wall like some common wench?"

She was so hot and wet for him, and it had been so long, Gwen didn't care. "However His Highness wants to give it to me."

He growled against her ear, the rumble starting low in his chest and seeming to emanate from deep in his bones.

Arthur broke away from her and bellowed into the hall, "Get out."

The revelers seemed to think he was kidding.

"I said, Get. Out." His voice thundered through the structure like some edict from God himself.

"Arthur, we can just go upstairs," she whispered.

"Oh no. You wanted here against the wall and that's where I'm giving it to you. But I'm done sharing any part of you. Do you understand?"

"Yes." Her knees were weak and she held onto him for support, his strong hands circled her waist.

Upon seeing who was in his arms, the revelers all made their exit, taking Dionysus's gift of wine with them.

"Where were we?"

Gwen found herself giddy and giggling. "Um, I think you were going to swive me against the wall like a camp follower."

"That I was." His voice was low and deep, his gaze focused on her mouth.

He dipped his head, kissing her hard. None of that gentle reverence like before. None of that fear that she'd break. She wasn't a damsel in distress any longer.

Well, not any kind of distress she didn't want. Gwen was most certainly distressed by the ache between her thighs, the longing, the raw need. It cut her like a razor.

His mouth was so hard and demanding, and those deliciously strong and callused hands slid from her waist to under her dress. He gripped both thighs and hoisted her up against the wall.

She locked her ankles around his hips and pushed her hands up under his shirt, palms tracing a familiar topography of healed wounds, scars from the whip, and the final one where Mordred pierced his side with a killing blow.

Even though she was so wet for him, even though she wanted him with every fiber of her being, she couldn't shut off her brain. She couldn't stop thinking about all the things she'd done wrong and all the chances lost to them.

It had been Vivienne and Morgan who'd brought him to Avalon, to the Summer Land where he would live forever.

And it had been in Morgan's arms where he'd found comfort, his cheek upon her breast, and her hands upon his brow when the wound fever was on him.

Finally, Gwen was able to just be grateful that he hadn't had to face the dark alone. Finally, she was able to admit that despite everything, she still loved Arthur Pendragon.

Lance had been a girlhood obsession. He'd been a

dream forced to live the real and that had crushed them both. Even though she'd been married to Arthur, Lance had been her first love, and all the angst and longing that went along with it.

It had been everything that many women dreamt of now. He was her Champion, he fought her battles, professed his undying devotion, wrote poetry that compared her to the sun and moon, and defended her with his life. It had been perfect. Until they'd tried to make it something more. Lancelot was a fantasy, and Arthur was reality.

But he was kind of a fantasy too.

He was everything Lancelot was, but more. He never betrayed anyone to get what he wanted.

And he was the forever love.

Gwen would always love Lance for who and what he'd been, for their time together, she could look at that now and while she still regretted the pain they caused each other, she didn't regret loving him.

She had for a long time.

But her passion, and the love of her woman's heart, it belonged to Arthur.

"Did you change your mind?" he whispered against her ear.

Gwen realized she'd been lost in her thoughts. Even with her cleft so ready for him, the wild need pulsing through her whole body, it was her stupid heart that captained the ship.

"No," she answered. "I want this more than anything, Arthur."

"Anything? More than gelato?"

She laughed again, but tears gathered behind her eyes, damn them. "More than gelato."

Because this would be the last time. She wanted Arthur to be free of her. Free of his pain. And Aphrodite could do that.

He wouldn't want her anymore. Or if he did, it would be the last time it would be like this: about love.

She'd made herself right with it because finally, she could fix everything.

But this one time, she'd take this memory for herself.

He pressed his forehead down to hers. "I don't know how to do this."

Gwen found herself giggling again. "I think you know how to do it very well. Women from all dimensions come to Avalon to... come." Her giggle merged into a nervous titter.

"No, I didn't care about them. You know I still love you. I don't want to hurt you."

"I'm no maiden, Arthur." She tittered again and hated the sound. "Well, maybe I am. It's been more than a century since I've had sex with anyone but myself."

He groaned. "That's a scene I'd like to see."

Heat flared. "You can have anything you want."

"What I want, Gwen, what I really want, is for you to be doing this because you want me. Me, not just someone because Lance is gone."

His words were daggers, but she understood why he'd flung them. It was a reasonable assumption to think she just didn't want to be alone. "Lance was gone a long time before he actually moved out. Does that make sense?"

He looked away from her, but yet his dick was still hard and he still held her up against the wall with no effort. She tried not to squirm against him, but then decided to let her body do as it wanted. He needed to feel her desire.

"I can feel how much you want me, can't you feel the same? How hot I am? How soaked my panties are?"

She licked her lips before continuing. "If I just wanted someone, there are any number of men on this island who'd fuck me in a second. And if I was just being perverse, Mordred is one of them. But no, Arthur. It's you between my thighs, and you I want there."

"Here, against the wall?"

"Anywhere."

"I've fucked any number of women against this wall. Let me take you to bed." He exhaled heavily. "*Our* bed."

Gwen thought that his reverence, his tenderness would be—she didn't know how to describe it. That there wouldn't be this fire. But she was wrong. It burned just as hot whether he was pulling her hair or speaking of gentler things.

"Yes."

He carried her up the stairs, the same as he had when the original castle had been built in Camelot. She hid her face in his neck, inhaled the scent of him. Loved the feel of his flexed muscles under her hand.

And suddenly, she was nervous. All of that *I am Badass and Powerful Hear Me Roar* gumption was gone. She could only think of all the women he'd been with. All of them with perfect bodies. With bigger breasts, smaller hips, and tighter asses.

Gwen reminded herself that she was the only one he'd ever had in this bed. She was the one he chose and he knew what her body looked like and he kept feeding her gelato anyway.

"After all these years, Gwen, are you afraid?" His voice was kind, gentle, the same as it had been on their wedding night. Goddess, but she loved this man so much it was an ache in her chest.

As usual, he knew what she was feeling. "Only that

when you unwrap me, I won't be the present you thought I was."

"Gwen, if you were in Lance's body, I'd still want this with you."

"That's kind of sexy." She smiled into his neck, remembering her pegging fantasy. "What about if I was Percivale?"

"Even then."

"What about if I was Medusa?"

"I might have to put a bag over your head so I don't die, but yeah. Even then."

She sobered. "What if I was Aphrodite?" This was how she could start the conversation.

"No more talking." He kicked open the door and lay her on the bed. His fingers made quick work of her dress and she was naked before she had a chance to argue.

She was sure her blush covered her entire body. Gwen felt like a virgin again.

"You're as beautiful as I remember."

"You're right. No more talking." She'd screw it up if there was. Gwen pulled him down to her and the weight of his body was as familiar to her as it was foreign. It was a strange sensation for everything to feel new and old at the same time.

No, not old. Old implied it was something passé, something well-used, and while she recognized she'd experienced it before, it was new. Because she wanted him to touch her, wanted to drown in him.

When she's first come to Arthur, she'd been a trembling and angry virgin. She didn't appreciate everything he had to offer her. They could've been happy.

Regret, shame, and longing filled her.

But she'd decided not to think about those things. Right

now was for this moment, not all the things that had come before.

"It hurts to look at you, Gwen. You're so beautiful." He whispered against her skin.

She tilted her lips up to his, because while it may have hurt to look at her, it hurt her to hear it. "Make love to me, Arthur."

"Forever." He kissed her throat. "Always."

# CHAPTER
# TWENTY-THREE

MORGAN

O n the walk back from the resort, Morgan knew
something had changed.

Shit, who was she kidding? *Everything* had
changed.

Her power grew by leaps and bounds, she had knowledge and access to things she'd never had before. Things
only the Lady of the Lake should have.

Morgan had always known she was Vivienne's heir, but
being immortal, she didn't expect to ever actually get
the job.

Of course, she never expected to have Lance either.

Her life was almost perfect. Except she knew it was like
balancing glass bubbles on the eye of a needle. In moments,
everything would shatter.

She used her new magick first to reach out for Vivienne.
Vivienne had always been like a mother to her and Morgan
had to know that she was okay.

Morgan was relieved to sense that she was. Then she

reached out to sense Lance.

He wasn't okay. He was afraid for Gwen, afraid of hurting Morgan, and afraid of facing Arthur. She stopped walking. If she didn't go back The Witch's Brew, she could pretend Lance was hers for just a few moments longer. She could float on this cloud of all the impossible, beautiful things.

Morgan was a realist and that set her feet back in motion toward the Brew. Toward Lance.

And toward the end of her happiness.

She opened the door and watched the play of expressions on his face that ran the gamut from surprise to concern.

Lance was Avalon born, of course he'd recognize the magick of the Lady of the Lake.

"Vivenne, my mother, is she…"

"I don't know how it happened. I need to talk to her, but my magick tells me she's okay."

His jaw flexed. "You wear it well."

"Thank you." The silence after she spoke was awkward and heavy. Morgan was used to being the one who stood quiet and disapproving, making everyone around her squirm. Instead, she was the one standing here, palms itchy, and a million words on her tongue, but not given breath.

"I can't do this, Morgan." He blurted.

Yes, he gave voice to all the doubts that pounded in her head like a bass drum.

"I know." Her voice didn't reverberate with all the authority of Avalon, it was a choked whisper, like that of a woman with a broken heart.

"It's not you."

"Isn't it?" She swallowed, choking down all of her

emotion. She'd could puke it up later where he wouldn't see her crying. "But it's okay. We both knew this was temporary."

"I still want you, I want to be with you, Morgan. But... my mother destroyed me. Destroyed Arthur. Gwen. Camelot. And for what? Because she was Lady of the Lake? I just... I can't."

Morgan lifted her chin. The noble Lancelot would never ask her to abdicate her power, not in so many words. But that's what he was doing. "No one asked you to."

"Aren't you? Standing there with that well of pain in your eyes?"

"Please." She stiffened her spine and pulled down the cloak of her power so he couldn't see her soft, aching places. "I've lived my life in service the same as you, Lance. I already told you I don't need a knight in shining armor. I *am* the Lady of the Lake. I would never give that up for a man. Even a man like you." Morgan meant to stop there, she did. But the words kept coming. "And that's what you do, isn't it? For the longest time, I thought this whole mess was Gwen's fault. I told her before you even slept together that if she made a man betray his vows, he'd resent her. But it wasn't just her. You need the woman in your life to give up everything for you. Guinevere was a queen. But you weren't happy until she had nothing but you. Then you left her. Is that because of Vivienne? Poor little Lancelot never felt as loved as Avalon so he has to break women because of his mommy issues. Well, you may have broken Vivienne's heart, you have broken Guinevere's but you will not break me." Lightning crackled at her fingertips.

"You're right." He nodded slowly. "The three of you are all the same. I, like your own son, was born only to serve Avalon," he spat. "My mother put Avalon first, Gwen put

Lyonesse first, then Arthur, then Camelot, there was always something more important than me. And now you too. I'm sick of serving."

"Lance, I don't think you've ever served anyone but yourself. Everything you've done has been to feed your own needs."

"And what about Avalon?" he roared.

It wasn't the sound, or the violence that made Morgan flinch, but his pain.

"What about it?" she managed, her calm tone masking the tide of emotions that swelled inside of her.

"What does Avalon serve? All of this sacrifice, all of this pain, and what is it for? The delusion of women with magick in their blood? A place to put the blame when you do things, horrible things, so you don't have to feel guilty. My mother brought down Camelot because she wanted to. Not for anything higher purpose than her own wants. Because she loved Arthur."

"No." Vivienne would never...

"Ask her. How else do you think I got Guinevere on the island and her immortality? I threatened to tell him."

"Even if Vivienne did what you say, that doesn't absolve you of your sin, Lance. No matter what anyone else did, you still chose your own actions."

"I suppose I did. Even that time I fucked Elaine because I thought she was Guinevere. No one else had any hand in that but me, huh? You witches and your damned magick." His face curled in snarls and pain.

"I don't deny my part in that. I never have." She exhaled slowly, using the pause to gather her strength. "I'm sorry you're still so angry with me." Her apology seemed to deflate him. "I'm sorry if my new position is unacceptable to you and I'm sorry that I won't give it up." She reached out to touch his face, but he jerked away like he'd been burned. "I do love you, Lance. But I knew you would never love me from the first time my stupid heart fluttered when you smiled at me."

He closed his eyes, but she didn't try to touch him again.

"And I definitely know it now, because when you love someone, you don't ask them to change. You're hurt, and I'm—" She didn't want to admit her heart had shattered in her chest. He didn't need to know that. Morgan had broken enough of her own rules by telling him that she loved him. "We both knew this would end. It doesn't have to end badly, Lance."

"Morgan—" She could hear the shame in his voice.

"We'll forget these few days ever happened, okay?" Morgan would never, *ever* forget them. Not even if she dug the memories out of her head with a spoon.

"I'm glad it's going to be that easy for you."

Part of her wanted to blurt her confession again, but she couldn't give him any more ammo to use against her. He just didn't like that she'd be able to move on without him. No one liked to hear that.

She didn't know what else to say to him, so she said, "You can stay in the guest room as long as you like."

"Really, Morgan? You can just shut it off?"

"What do you want me to do?" she cried. "You want me to break because you don't want to fuck me anymore? That's never going to happen." But it was, right now, everything in her that could crack, break, or shatter was being ground to ash and dust.

"I just want to know I wasn't the only one who felt something. That it was real."

"It was real, Lance."

"Gwen said something to me the night I left. She said I was no knight in shining armor. I was a douchebag in tinfoil. I think she's right."

Lance walked past her, careful not to touch her.

And whatever had lived and breathed between them left with him.

For all of Morgan's posturing, she was broken. She wanted Vivienne. Her wisdom, her strength, her guidance. Morgan could be Lady of the Lake, but she still needed the only mother figure she'd ever known.

She transported herself to Vivienne's cottage and saw Vivienne laughing with Hector. She was sitting on a fallen tree, and the knight's reposed position, back against the trunk spoke of an intimacy Morgan had so recently lost. Her face flushed, her eyes bright. Yes, Vivienne was much more than okay. Shedding the mantle of the Lady of the Lake seemed to bring her to vibrant life.

Vivienne looked up and the flush on her cheeks disappeared. Knowledge infused the other woman and she held her arms open.

Morgan didn't care that Hector was there, didn't care that he'd see her break, she didn't care about anything but the comfort and safety Vivienne offered.

Morgan melted into a puddle, her head in Vivienne's lap and her arms wrapped around her waist.

"Should I kill someone for you?" Hector offered helpfully.

Vivienne spoke softly. "Don't kill him. He's my son after all. Give us about an hour and then bring him here."

"As you wish."

That was when the floodgates opened and Morgan cried.

She hadn't cried since Mordred was born and she knew

what pain and suffering lay in store for him.

Her tears were hot and acidic, they burned down her face, but they did nothing to assuage the ache inside of her. Morgan didn't know anything could hurt like this.

Vivienne smoothed her hand over her hair and down her back and crooned soft words to her.

"Let it out, little one. It's all going to be okay."

"I'm sorry," she hiccupped. Damn it, she couldn't stop saying it, worse, she couldn't stop feeling it.

"You're human, Morgan. You're allowed to have feelings."

"I knew he wouldn't love me, I knew, and I did it anyway." She promised herself she wouldn't do this, wouldn't be this...

"I know." Vivienne stroked her hair until the shuddering stopped and the tidal wave of tears had dried.

Vivienne's hands were cool on her heated face as she smoothed her fingers over her forehead and cheeks. The steady, gentle rhythm and Vivienne's quiet song in her head was what finally helped her find her center and let her breathe again.

It always had. When they'd come for her, Morgan hadn't wanted to leave her village, her mother. But Vivienne had extended her hand and upon taking it, Morgan felt like she finally belonged.

She sniffed, trying to dismiss the storm of emotion. "My first act of Lady of the Lake was to sob into your dress like a child."

"Actually, you brought a storm to Avalon. It's been so long since I've seen one."

The clouds overhead were dark and angry, Morgan's pain having manifested in thunder, lightning, and when fat drops began to fall, Vivienne laughed.

"I'm screwing everything up."

"Not at all, Morgan. Things are changing. Maybe with me, it was only allowed to rain after dark. With you, it can be anything you wish. If I can offer you one piece of advice, it would be to remember you are not Avalon."

"But you always said..."

"I was wrong. And there's a lot for me to fix, my girl. Starting with my idiot son." She sighed. "After my idiot self, of course."

Morgan dropped her head back into Vivienne's lap, the rain falling everywhere but on them.

"You don't have to do anything to Lance. He's hurting too."

"He's been fighting this so long. He was always supposed to end up with you." Vivienne's hand paused mid-stroke. "I think that's my fault."

Morgan looked up at her. "Why? Because of what Lance said? That you brought Camelot down because you wanted Arthur?"

Vivienne nodded her head, a silent confession.

For some reason, this calmed Morgan and she sat up, taking Vivienne's hand in her own. "I know you, Vivienne. If you wanted Arthur, you wouldn't have felled a kingdom just to have him. Even if you've convinced yourself that you did. Mortal society rules have never applied to us. You were the damn Lady of the Lake and if you wanted a king, you'd have him."

Vivienne's expression warmed further. "Couldn't the same be said of you and my son?"

"That's different."

"Isn't it always?" Vivienne said kindly.

"I love him, Vivienne. I always have. I think I always will."

"That is as it should be. I know he loves you. He was infatuated with Gwen for so long. He never really loved her." Vivienne sighed. "Oh, I guess he did, but in the way a boy loves a girl. Infatuation. That first puppy love is what they call it now. But love of a man for a woman? That's all yours, Morgan. I raised my son to be certain things. Good and bad, because there is both in all of us. But he can't accept that you have more power than he does. It makes him feel useless."

"I can't be what I'm not."

"And he better not ask you to, either. But Morgan, when he figures it out, are you still going to want him? I don't want either of you to hurt this way."

"Yes." Morgan nodded emphatically. "I've never wanted anyone more."

"And that's why you won't enchant him and take him. That's why I wouldn't have done that to Arthur."

"No, and you wouldn't have crushed him either."

"So much for all the wicked witch theories, eh?" Vivienne eyed her knowingly.

"Yeah, well, I have a rep and street cred I need to keep."

"Now, you're the Lady of the Lake. You don't need any street cred."

"We're quite the pair, aren't we?" Morgan sniffed.

"I suppose we are."

"So tell me about Hector."

Vivienne's cheeks colored. "I. um. Well, he was on my personal guard. And I used him as he was intended."

"He's more to you than that, Vivienne."

"He's Lance's best friend, for goddess's sake. I don't know what I'm doing."

"Falling in love." Then Morgan remembered that Vivienne didn't know Aphrodite was on the island. Well, she

SARANNA DEWYLDE

would just keep that to herself. Vivienne would automatically assume anything that Hector felt for her wouldn't be real. Aphrodite would never do that. As pissed off as Aphrodite was about Vivienne using love as a curse, she wouldn't turn around and do the same thing.

Plus, Aphrodite was her friend and she knew that Morgan loved Vivienne like a mother.

"That's just stupid, now, isn't it?" Vivienne whispered. "I shouldn't fall in love with a boy."

"He's not a boy, Vivienne."

"I guess I know that. I suppose it's my turn to look to the Lady of the Lake for her wisdom. Will you give us your blessing, Morgan?"

Morgan thought she was going to cry all over again. Next thing she knew, she'd be hanging out with Gwen, shoe-shopping and eating gelato. All decidedly un-Morgan like girly things. It was like an infection.

"Of course." She drew Vivienne in and Morgan brushed her lips across her forehead to mimic the blessing of the goddess and spoke, "May all of the bounty and blessings of Avalon follow you both for all of your days." Morgan was inspired to add a wish of her own. "And when he says he loves you, I wish you the courage to admit that you love him not only to him, but to yourself."

Vivienne colored again and glanced down at her hands. "You're going to be an excellent Lady."

Morgan's heart was still broken, and deep down inside part of her still felt like the world was ending. But seeing to her duties as Lady of Lake filled something blank and empty. It warmed her.

Even if Lance never loved her, she knew what it was to love. To surrender herself. And she realized that's what Avalon had been waiting on for both her and Vivienne.

# TWENTY-FOUR

APHRODITE

Aphrodite wasn't sure about this whole turning into a dragon thing. She rather liked her skin, sans scales, and she was worried it was going to give her hairs on her chin. She'd always heard wise dragons had beards, and Aphrodite liked to think of herself as wise, but she'd rather remain beardless.

But, she supposed she could try it. She was on vacation after all. If she screwed it up too badly, Hera could fix it for her.

She closed her eyes and imagined the prettiest dragon she could. When she opened her eyes, the rest of the world had gotten a lot bigger.

That couldn't be good.

Aphrodite looked down at herself.

She was pink.

And sparkly.

Not necessarily a bad thing. Her scales had a kind of abalone shimmer. She could hang with that.

She took a step forward and fell flat, snout first into the sand.

Sand up her nose was almost as bad as sand in her bits. *Almost.* The worst tickle made her snout twitch and she shook her head, trying to dislodge the tiny granules of sand.

No luck.

She sneezed, blowing sand, and fire out of her nose.

Something popped in her back.

Aphrodite decided she was much too old for this kind of nonsense.

"Well, who are you?" A deep voice rumbled with mirth.

She tried to turn her head, but found she couldn't. Her stupid wing had unfurled and gotten caught on her horns when she sneezed.

This was so humiliating.

Aphrodite found herself scooped up by warm hands that gently untangled her from her own wing. She blinked owlishly and found herself staring up at Aeron.

*Hey, put me down.* But instead, only a faint mewling sound came out of her snout.

"Such a lovely little hatchling, aren't you?" He scratched under her chin as he cooed at her.

*Oh please, Zeus, don't let it be hairy*, she begged as she tilted into the scratch. It really was very nice. Finally, she managed another sound besides the mewling. It was only a purr, but it was better than mewling.

She sighed, and fire shot out of her nostrils again, singing his fingers.

"Aphrodite?" He held her up above his head. "I'd recognize that singe anywhere. What did you do?"

She shrugged her shoulders and blinked.

"If you were trying to entice me, not so much. I'm not

on the playground extraction team, if you know what I mean."

Aphrodite huffed and singed him again.

"Be nice, or I won't help you change back."

But even as he spoke, her body was once again her own and her arms were wrapped around his neck. "It was an accident."

"That was for my benefit, though, wasn't it? Come on, admit it."

"So what if it was?" She shifted against him.

"Did Morgan tell you to do it? I'm going to get that witch. Paybacks are a—"

"Yes, yes, and more yes. I've decided I'm not on board with this whole friend thing. I want the dragon." She would have stomped her foot if she'd been standing.

"Aphrodite, you're trying too hard."

"Excuse me?" Love wouldn't be denied. And Aphrodite didn't care much for how it felt either. Rather like when Morgan told her that Ares just wasn't that into her.

He laughed. "Look, if you were just another goddess looking to get back at her ex, I'd have no problem giving you exactly what you want. But I'm not putting my heart on the line when yours isn't."

"How do you know it's not?" Aphrodite said, looking at his mouth and thinking about kissing him.

"Because you're still trying to punish Ares."

"No, I'm not. He's supposed to end up with Morrigan. I've accepted that. My power, my goddesshood, it won't let me do anything else."

"But what about your heart? Everyone has heard the tales of Aphrodite and Ares. I mean, you're still pissed about The War That Cannot Be Named. If you were over him, you'd be able to let go of that."

She narrowed her eyes. "I could make you, you know."

He eased Aphrodite to her feet, his arms still wrapped around her. "You won't."

"How do you know I won't?" She rested her palms on his shoulders and of their own volition, her fingers traced the outline of the dragon. It shifted under his skin, and Aphrodite shivered.

"Because you didn't do it to Ares after millennia."

"Maybe I learned my lesson." She wouldn't, but she didn't like being predictable.

He closed his eyes and held himself still as she continued to explore the shifting planes of his body.

"What did you say about using love as a weapon? And that's what you'd be doing. You'd be using me to hurt Ares and to soothe your wounded ego."

Damn. He was right.

"I can't argue with that, but doesn't this feel good?"

"If we did everything that felt good, then where would we be?" His voice was light and teasing, but when he opened his eyes and looked at her, she saw a wealth of sorrow.

And Aphrodite, for all of her plans and plotting, her short temper and smiting, she was a forgiving creature. Because Love forgives. Love is kind. She couldn't bear to add to his pain. Especially not when he was so unlike any of the other gods she knew.

"I'm sorry." She dropped her hands to her sides. "I don't want to hurt you. That was never my intention."

He didn't release her. "I know." His skin continued to shift as the dragon inside of him clawed toward the surface, sought out her touch. It spoke to her almost as clearly as Aeron himself. It projected its needs and wants into her brain like an oil painting. It wanted the same thing

Aphrodite did, to be lost in sensation, touch and pleasure. But it wanted her for forever, not just for tonight.

Aeron laughed uncomfortably. Then his eyes narrowed as some awareness washed over him. "What *did* you intend to do?"

"What are you talking about?"

"The island has been in an uproar since you got here, Aphrodite. There's power zinging everywhere and everything is falling apart. As soon as you got here, Lance left Gwen, Arthur made it an actual crime for the market to run out of gelato, Morgan, your friend, became Lady of the Lake after you cursed Vivienne. And now you're chasing me and pretending you want me more than Ares. Is that to keep me distracted while you wreak havoc on my island?"

Aphrodite blinked. "Have you lost your mind?" Her tone wasn't one of incredulity, but of genuine concern.

"I'm a war god. Did you think I wouldn't see what you were up to? Strategy is my bread and butter."

The goddess arched a brow. "Perhaps you don't remember our discussion in the meadow. *You* sought *me* out, not the other way around. I was in the middle of dealing with Vivienne because she trespassed in *my* realm. I agreed to your request because it was the right thing to do. Not because I'm afraid of you. And that would be the only reason I'd try to manage you with sex." She sighed. "You're more like Ares than I thought. You war gods are all the same. Nothing can simply be what it is. There's always some ulterior motive."

She turned away from him.

"That's because there always *is* an ulterior motive." He grabbed her arm again. "Admit that you just wanted to piss Ares off."

"Of course I did. That's what we do, but I told you, I'd

finished with that. And I understand why you don't believe me. We've already beat this to death and I get it. But now you're accusing me of manipulating you for...for what, exactly?"

"To move Morgan to the seat of power. To take everything away from Vivienne because she pissed you off. Everyone knows the story of the golden apples and what happened to the men who didn't choose you."

Aphrodite's mouth fell open. "Are you serious? Morgan is the Lady of the Lake because that's what the magick of Avalon decreed. She was always Vivienne's heir. Arthur made it illegal for the market to run out of gelato because Gwen loves gelato. He's never stopped loving her. And she didn't realize she loved him until now. Vivienne has learned her lesson and now she's fighting for her happy ever after. Yes, sometimes my presence can exacerbate matters of love, but I've done nothing wrong. All I've done is try to take a vacation and figure out my own life. And I've learned a few things."

"What have you learned?"

"That I should never date war gods. Because on the surface, no matter how polite they are, how charming, how funny, deep inside, they aren't more than their office. You say that War and Slaughter are not you, that they're just part of your job, but you see subterfuge where there is none. Just like Ares. Just like all the other war gods that I've known."

"You're not perfect, Aphrodite. Have you ever stopped to consider that War does have its place, just like Love?"

"That's where you're wrong." She jerked away from him, her power singing him as she went.

"Now you're just angry I've turned you down. What are you going to do? Smite all of Avalon?" he said quietly.

She stared at him hard for a long moment. "You don't know me or Love at all." Aphrodite willed herself to appear back at her cottage. She was ready to go home. She'd had enough of this "vacation" and Avalon.

Aphrodite started packing, zapping things back to her house on Olympus.

A deep voice rumbled from the doorway. "Finally coming to your senses?"

She looked up and saw Ares standing there. Aphrodite didn't have it in her to go another round with him. She was tired of fighting. Tired of wanting something that didn't belong to her.

She'd had enough.

Aphrodite sat down on the bed. "Yes, I think I have."

But he didn't say anything smug. He surprised her. He sat down on the bed next to her and he put his arm around her.

"I never wanted you to be hurt."

"I know." And she did. Ares had never been malicious. Win at any cost, yes. But he never set out to hurt her because he'd never believed she could be hurt. He'd accepted her as his equal in all ways. She supposed that should've been a comfort to her.

"Are you hurt?"

His warmth was comforting and familiar—part of her wanted to lean into him and forget everything that had happened these past few days. But she couldn't do that. She'd seen his future and it wasn't with her.

"My pride, maybe." That was a teensy, tiny lie. Her heart hurt. But being Love, she knew it wouldn't be forever.

"What can I do? Should I kill him? I can, you know."

She rewarded him with a small laugh. "No. But here's what you can do. Don't come see me—"

"Are we back to this?" He wasn't moaning and groaning, or chiding her. It was a serious question.

"It's where we need to be. I wasn't kidding when I said I looked. Your future is with Morrigan. Not me."

He snorted. "Mori? Not likely. She's like me if I had a vagina. If I wanted to date myself, I would."

"You haven't looked close enough. Of course she's like you. She's a goddess of war. But she's also the Goddess of Hearth. She has a woman's softness, a woman's wants and needs. She just doesn't show them to you because they're soft and vulnerable, and you're nothing if not a tactician."

He exhaled heavily. "I don't want her." He said this slowly, as if that's all it would take to make Aphrodite understand.

"Maybe not now, but you will. And when you do," she paused, choking back emotion. "Know that you join with her with my blessing." Aphrodite pulled away from him and fought to keep from wrapping her arms around him and clinging not only to Ares, but to her past, to what she knew was safe.

"You mean this," he said, surprised.

"Please go now."

"Don't ask me not to never see you again. I couldn't stand it. Whether you want to be or not, you're a part of me, and I'm part of you."

It was the nicest, most romantic thing he'd ever said to her. Too bad it had to come at the end, rather than the beginning.

"That won't change. You're the father of my children, Ares. I'll always love you. But we don't belong together. Give me, and yourself time to heal. Maybe we can have brunch in a hundred years or something." She had to fight not to cry.

She thought of Gwen and how she hadn't had sex or love in the last hundred years and Aphrodite thought her future looked awfully fucking bleak at the moment.

"I do love you, Aphrodite. I know you never believed that." His weight pushing down the bed next to her seemed like the heaviest thing in the cosmos.

"I know. But you're not *in* love with me. Maybe you were once when we were godlings."

"I don't want to leave. I know when I walk out the door, it's done. We've never been able to be done."

She laughed and it was a tinny sound.

"Maybe you could throw something at me for old time's sake?"

"You know if I do that, we'll end up in bed."

"Well, *technically*, we're already in bed," he teased.

Zeus, why did this have to be so hard? She sniffed. "Please, just...please."

Then the weight was gone, as was Ares, and the life she'd always thought she'd have. Aphrodite didn't want to cry, she knew it was for the best for both of them, but she couldn't help mourning the loss of what she thought had been her Happily Ever After.

CHAPTER

# TWENTY-FIVE

VIVIENNE

After Morgan left, Vivienne had just managed to compose herself when Hector appeared as promised, hauling her recalcitrant son with him.

Lance looked back and forth between them and arched a brow. "Really?"

"Really what?" She put her hands on her hips, as if she didn't know exactly what.

"I was going to tell you, but I thought you had enough on your plate." Hector shrugged, unabashed. "You're my best friend, Lance. So keep a civil tongue in your head. I don't want to have to kick your ass."

Lance sighed. "I haven't been training, so you probably could."

"Probably?" Hector snorted. "I know I could."

"You were always the better choice for the noble knight schtick."

"And you were the spoiled son, so spoiled and indulged, he never learned what love is," Vivienne said softly.

"Vivienne—" Lance began.

"Maybe today, you could call me mother?" She asked carefully.

"Look, I've already had a bad day."

"I know. Morgan's been to see me."

"And you're taking me to task for upsetting your perfect, precious Morgan?" He crossed his arms over his chest.

Vivienne eyed him. She really wanted to smack him in the back of the head. "Hector, can you give us a moment. We'll be fine."

Hector nodded and went inside her cottage.

"You're my mother. I don't need that guy telling me whether I can or can't talk to you," Lance growled.

"That guy? He's your best friend."

"And you're sleeping with him. So he's now *that* guy."

"Yes, I am. But that's not why we're here."

"Right. Morgan. The new Lady of the Lake," he sneered.

"Name something you wanted that I didn't give you," Vivienne demanded.

"Your love. I wanted you to put me before Avalon. Just once."

She sighed. It was long, drawn out, and much put upon. "I didn't kill Guinevere."

"That's because I wouldn't let you."

"Do you really think a knight, even one so blessed and Avalon born as yourself, could stop the magick of the Lady of the Lake? The oracle said it was supposed to happen the same way the stories say it *did* happen. You were supposed to save her, but only to take her to a monastery. You were supposed to end up with Morgan. Do you have any idea how angry I was when you showed up dragging Guinevere's whey-face behind you?"

"I'd say the lightning bolt to the back of the head adequately expressed your feelings."

"And I could have incinerated her then. I could have incinerated her when she was tied to the stake. The people of Camelot would've thought it was a righteous act of their new god. But I didn't. Because you loved her. At every turn, you thwarted me and Avalon, and at every turn, I chose you. My son."

"You wanted Arthur." Lance looked down at the ground.

"Yes, I did. I don't deny that. And for the longest time, I felt so much guilt for everything I'd done. But I did the best I could with the resources I had." Vivienne exhaled heavily, and with the expulsion of air came the expulsion of guilt. She spoke of it, and it was like blowing out a candle.

"Why couldn't you just have been my mother?" He spoke slowly, his voice full of emotion.

"Because I'm not. There is more to me, to any woman, than simply Lancelot's mother. Guinevere was more than just the king's wife. And Morgan is more than simply Lancelot's woman." She grabbed her son's face firmly between her hands and forced him to look up at her. "That doesn't mean that being your mother isn't the thing I'm most grateful for, the most proud of, or that I don't love you more than the breath in my body. I would die for you, kill for you, and live for you, but I am a person that exists outside of your control. We all are. The same as you are more than a champion. You are a man. You have a heart, a mind, and a soul. You must become what you were meant to become."

Lance looked as if she'd slapped him. "I'm an asshole. That's what I've become."

Vivienne smiled. "I'm glad you see that. But no, there's

more. *You're* more. Don't forget the good things. You were a Knight of the Round Table, the Queen's Champion, you were the ideal. Your imperfections make you human, Lancelot."

He grimaced. "They make me unworthy. For so long, I was so pissed that everyone kept trying to make me out to be some hero and I'm not. I never was. And that cut so deep, I just stayed angry. At everyone. You, Arthur, Gwen... and Morgan. Especially Morgan. I don't deserve her. Especially not after how I treated her. The things I've said, not just today, but over centuries." His broad shoulders slumped.

Vivienne couldn't help but laugh. Not at her son's pain, never that. But that his very thinking made him all those things he thought he wasn't. "Do you think heroes ever know they're heroes? They shouldn't. That's when they'll find they're the villains of the story. You've made mistakes, we all have. But you're not a villain." She wrapped her arms around her son carefully, hopefully. He hadn't let her embrace him in years. Vivienne remembered holding him as a baby, his sweet apple-baby smell like all Avalon born, his sunshine curls on top of his head that tickled her nose, and the wonder that she'd created such a gloriously perfect creature. "And you do most definitely deserve Morgan, and she deserves you."

His arms tightened around her. "I'm sorry."

"Me too. I love you, Lance. I always have. More than anything."

"I'm not calling Hector dad," he mumbled against her hair.

Vivienne laughed and fought her tears. He'd forgiven her.

"But I love you, Mom. I will make all of this right. I will."

"I know."

He hugged her a little tighter. "How do you know?"

"Because you're Lancelot du Lac, my son, and knight in shining armor." Vivienne didn't want to break the hug, but she did. She stepped back from the man her son had become and smiled. "There is a new Lady of the Lake with no champion. You better get going so you can fix that."

"She said she doesn't need a champion."

"Maybe not, but you'll be her champion anyway." Vivienne thought of Hector, of all he'd done for her when she'd been so sure she didn't need him.

"If I'm supposed to respect that she's more than my woman, how can I demand to be her champion?"

Vivienne smiled brighter. "You'll see. Make the gesture, Lance. And it will all come together." She pursed her lips as the smile faded. "That is, if you feel it. Only if you feel it."

"I used to think she'd cast some kind of spell on me." He looked ashamed. "But I do feel it. I have for a long time." He sighed. "I've always been the one who had to be strong and I'm terrified of her strength. Gwen needed me, and Morgan, she doesn't need me. She doesn't need anyone or anything. She's like a tsunami."

"She doesn't need you, but she wants you and that's so much better."

"I really hope so. Hector said she'd been here. Do you know where she went?"

"To the orchards."

Lance didn't even say goodbye, he just took off running.

"I can come out now?" Hector emerged from her cottage, drinking an apple ale.

"Yes. Thank you for getting him to come see me. We haven't spoken like that in so long." Vivienne marveled at how much more confident she was now that she wasn't the Lady of the Lake.

"It does my heart good to see you smile, Vivienne. If I'd known that was all it took, I'd have dragged him kicking and screaming years ago."

"Everything happens in its own time." Yes, she admitted again, she felt so much wiser now that she wasn't wearing her mantle of guilt.

"It does." He nodded. "And I need to speak to Morgan about my vows. I can't be a member of her personal guard, Vivienne."

"I should hope not." Jealousy flared, but she tamped it down.

"Was that a spark of jealousy, my Lady?" Hector grinned.

"No," she lied.

His grin turned into a smirk. "Oh, I think it might be."

"Fine. I am. I'm jealous." Today seemed to be the day for admissions, so why stop with her guilt, and her fear? What about the good things, too? Not that jealousy was a good thing, but this flirtation with Hector was.

Since she'd acknowledged her secret feelings for Arthur, they'd been singed by the sunlight and they blackened and withered to ash. They'd never been all she made them out to be and it had been a kind of release for her to realize that.

He arched a brow. "What shall we do about that, Vivienne?"

"Nothing at all. I would prefer to continue on as we have been." She said it lightly, but she meant it.

"Would you?" he asked, pulling her close against him. "Really? Or are you just afraid of what it means that you're no longer Lady of the Lake?"

His tone wasn't accusatory. Vivienne knew that he was

trying to help her. So rather than be offended, or upset, she smiled. "Really. And if you want to wait to be sure that I'm sure, I understand. It's not like we don't have the rest of eternity." She touched his hand. "But we've both waited a long time to be happy already. I trusted you, trusted someone else's magick because you said it was okay. And it was. So now, I'd like it if you'd trust me."

"I always trust you, Vivienne. I'd be yours even if you just wanted to use me as a shield against the world. That's all I've ever known. That's my purpose."

"Maybe now, instead of being my shield, you could just love me?"

"I do, Vivinne."

For the first time in centuries, all was finally right with Vivienne du Lac, Former Lady of the Lake.

# TWENTY-SIX

## ARTEMIS

Artemis wanted to go home.

This vacation wasn't at all what she'd signed up for.

Everything hurt. Her legs, her arms, her thighs.

Her heart.

Mordred was right. She was feeling some strange movement in her chest and at first, she was sure she'd caught some kind of strange parasite. In a sense, she guessed that she had, but she knew the cure.

Artemis knew that distance would be the only thing that would kill this bug.

Or Aphrodite.

It wasn't love yet, but it would be, and Artemis just couldn't afford that. Mordred was her first. How dumb would it be to latch on to the first guy she let under her toga? Especially since he was like some carnival ride.

How long until he was bored with her charms? How long until the curse faded?

How long until he left her begging her best friend on her knees to rip her heart out of her chest like Hades had done when he released Persephone?

It was unacceptable.

She needed to get back to the house to pack.

Or screw it, she could just leave her stuff here. She didn't need it. She might miss the comb Poseidon had given her for her five-hundredth birthday, but she could get another.

"Have you had enough, then?" Mordred asked lazily when she squirmed away from him.

"Yes." No. She'd never get enough of him and that was the problem.

"Well, I do hope you'll leave me a good review on Yelp." He stood and used his magick to dress himself. "Arthur and I have a contest of sorts."

It seemed once it was consummated, the curse was broken. Artemis had to admit that there was some part of her that wanted him cursed. It made her feel safe. Like a warm wading pool that had been secluded from a turbulent, deep sea. If he loved her, he couldn't hurt her.

But here he was talking about what had happened between them like it was nothing more than a business transaction.

*Which is what you wanted, dummy. Don't go complaining now.*

Yes, it was exactly what she wanted. Artemis herself had told him no feelings.

"That's it, then?" she said in a clipped tone.

He paused and looked over at her. "That's what you wanted, right? You said you'd had enough. I assume I'm dismissed, Oh Goddess of the Hunt."

She swallowed hard. This wasn't what she wanted at all. No matter what she'd said. "Can we…"

"Can we do it again? If you like. You're on vacation and I am, after all, just a tourist attraction." He said this with no rancor, but his words were sharp nonetheless.

"No. Can we…talk?" She bit her lip. "Is that hopelessly stupid and virginal of me?" Artemis propped herself up on her elbow to look at him.

The hard lines of his face softened. Well, as soft as something chiseled from marble could be. "Maybe, a little. But if you want to talk, we can talk. I don't have any plans." He eased back down into the grass, elbows propped on his knees.

"You're supposed to say it's not stupid at all," she teased, feeling better that whatever had been between them before was back.

"How bored would we all be if I did everything I was supposed to do?"

"There is that," she acquiesced. "So how many women have you slept with?"

"Direct, aren't you?" He sounded bored, but she knew she was deflecting.

"We had this part of the discussion already. You already know that while I like the hunt and the chase, I like to be honest too. If you don't want to answer, it's not like I can make you. You could just say, 'fuck off, Artie' and that's what I'd do. I'd fuck off."

"Artie? I would never in a million years say 'fuck off, *Artie*.'" He made a face. "Artie is a fat garbage man from Omaha. You are the Goddess of the Hunt. You are *Artemis*." He snorted. "Artie." He said it again like it left a foul taste in his mouth.

It made her giggle. His incredulity, his palpable disgust, it was so out of place on his face that it tickled her.

"That's what Aphrodite has called me since I was born. Didn't you have a nickname?"

"Can you imagine my mother, the wicked witch, calling me anything but Mordred?" A black brow arched in query.

Artemis cocked her head to the side, studying him. "I don't know. Maybe. She was rather gentle with Lancelot."

"She's not grooming him to destroy a kingdom."

"No, it seems like he did that on his own." Artemis smiled. "I think I can see it. I bet you were her little crabapple or something equally endearing."

"She called me Little Prince. As if there were some danger of me forgetting I was the son of a king." His tone had dark undercurrents, but he wasn't sour.

"Maybe she didn't want you to forget that you are a son of Avalon. Like Lance. Isn't he a prince of sorts as well?"

"I'd rather not discuss him."

"Okay then, back to how many women you've had."

"Why does it matter?"

"I just want to know." Why was he being so difficult? It wasn't like a state secret or anything.

"And I ask again, why? You're a goddess, it's not like you can get an STD."

"Why is that the first place your brain goes?" She scowled. "Do you... I mean..." They hadn't discussed protection.

"No. I do not." He laughed.

"Then why won't you tell me? You know my brother is a total manwhore. It's not like you're going to shock me or anything."

"I don't know, okay?" He said this like he was confessing some grievous sin.

"Oh." She pursed her lips. Artemis had never stopped to wonder how he felt about his position on Avalon. She'd thought he was a manwhore and proud of it—most men would be. But century after century...

And here she was treating him the same way.

"Conversation killer right there, isn't it?" He leaned back in the grass and looked up at the sky.

"So, not knowing, it bothers you?" As soon as she spoke, she felt like an even bigger, steamier piece of minotaur crap. Why couldn't she just leave it alone? It was like kicking a dead Pegasus.

"Sometimes." He sighed. "Don't mistake me, I'm not having a pity Mordred party. I know what I am. I know what I'm good for. My place in the world. I have it better than some. Worse than others."

"I'm sorry about the curse. If I'd known, I wouldn't have kissed you."

"Why not?" It was his turn to roll over and study her.

"Because making you love me would be wrong." She wondered how he didn't see that.

He laughed. "I'd have kissed you anyway, Artemis. I wanted you from the moment I saw you. Curse be damned."

"But—"

"But what? After what I did to Circe and Medusa, I probably have it coming anyway. It's my turn to suffer. We all have them. Just like you broke my heart, someone will break yours. It happens. And we survive."

Artemis knew plenty of stories where the heartbroken hadn't survived. "Not everyone."

"Then this life wasn't for them anyway. Something my mother always told me is you can't appreciate the beauty of the stars without the darkness of night. Night was born to be black and it is what it is. It doesn't apologize, instead the stars burn bright in its arms."

She smiled, thinking of Nyx. Of all that great power she held within her, but her quiet, gentle nature. She'd said something similar once about her son Thanatos—Death. "So you're saying that you're the dark and Camelot was a star?"

"That's how my mother made it okay."

"Made what okay?" She asked, twirling a dandelion between her fingertips.

"Me."

His answer tore at her. He was much nobler a creature than she'd ever imagined. Thanatos wore his darkness like a cloak, and it looked good on him. Hades burned with dark poetry like Byron, but Mordred—

He was temptation and sin, an irresistible combination for any goddess worth her margarita salt. Mordred LeFay was the living, breathing epitome of a bad boy. He didn't know any other way to exist. She was screwed—oh so horribly screwed. In fact, she was fucked. Straight up fucked. Artemis had a weakness for the misunderstood bad boy, but the darkness in him that strived to be something it wasn't—this was devastating.

"Of course you're okay." Artemis managed. "Everything and everyone has a purpose. It's not always pretty, but it's necessary."

"Necessary evil, yes. I've heard it before."

"No, more than that. Like Morgan said, you need the night to see the stars. You need the night to grow. Living things can't survive with no reprieve from the sun. Apollo is a sun god and he married a titan. Nyx—the night and all things dark belong to her. Her son is Death, her daughter

Nightmares, and they are loved. Don't you know that no matter why you were born that your mother loved you?"

"In her own fashion. But it's not her love I want. It's yours. And I can't have it."

Artemis didn't know what to say.

"Not so keen on talking now, are you?"

"What do you want me to say, Mordred? You don't understand."

"Of course I do. You're my punishment."

"I don't want to be your punishment," she cried. "I already told you that I can have Aphrodite—"

"It's you who doesn't understand now." He brushed his fingers over hers. "It hurts, it hurts so damn good, Artemis. I've never felt like this before. I don't want it to go away. I always wanted to know what it was like to love someone more than myself. Now I do. For all the fucking I've done, my heart was still virgin."

Oddly enough, she understood what he meant. It resonated inside of her and made her wonder if that's what she should do, if she should surrender to these budding feelings and let them grow wild. Or run away as far and fast as she could and never think about him again.

"Your curse—"

"Leave it alone, Artemis."

"What if I want you to love me without it?" She squeaked. *Stupid traitorous mouth. It wasn't supposed to say that out loud.*

"I wouldn't. I can't."

"So it's not real. Why would you want that for yourself? And if you love me, why would want it for me?"

"That's the beauty of it. I didn't see that until now. But the fact that I can't have you makes it that much sweeter."

"I'm glad it's going to work out for you." Artemis replied in a tone that said she thought anything but.

"You already said you didn't want feelings."

"I don't, but I had them anyway. Guess that doesn't matter."

"Shit, Artemis." He leaned back in the grass. "When the curse is broken, or it fades, I'll go back to being the same dick I was when I was okay being a carnival ride. Run now. Go back to Olympus and have Aphrodite root me out of your heart like a weed."

"I will. I'll do just that." Artemis stood and walked away from the clearing, tears burning in her eyes.

She'd meant to only play her V-Card, not her heart. It was time to cut her losses and run.

# CHAPTER
# TWENTY-SEVEN

GWEN

G wen lay sated and warm in Arthur's arms, but she was not happy.

She knew the next words that came out of her mouth would shatter their idyll, but she owed it to Arthur to offer him a reprieve from his pain. From everything she'd done to wrong him.

"Regrets already?" he whispered, though his tone was not unkind.

"Not for today, no."

"Then why are you so stiff in my arms?" He dragged his cheek against hers, the soft scrape of goatee against her skin making her shiver as the sensation reminded her that just moments ago, he'd been doing that same thing between her thighs. "You should be snoring."

"I don't snore."

"Yes, you do. You sound like a piglet with a head cold."

"I do not!" she gasped. "Ladies do not snore."

He laughed. "But you do, and it's adorable. I didn't realize I'd miss it until you left."

She thought about all of the little things that she'd never noticed about him until he was no longer hers. The way his eyes crinkled when he laughed, the way his dirty clothes were never on the floor, and how he never failed notice her.

"There's that heavy exhale again. Say what's on your mind, Gwen."

"Aphrodite is on the island."

"I knew that."

"Did she come to see you?" Gwen asked, biting her lip and girding herself for the answer. She knew that she was hiding from Ares, was it possible that she'd come to see the sights and do *all* of the touristy things? Gwen knew she had no right to be jealous, but she was.

"No, I just heard some of my guests talking about her and Aeron."

"Oh." She was silent again for a long moment. "She's agreed to help us."

"Help us? What sort of help do we need from the Goddess of Love?" Arthur pulled her more tightly against him.

Goddess, but she loved the way he smelled. The hardness of his body. The way she fit against him. Gwen was having trouble finding the words—no wait, they were there. Her mouth just didn't want to speak them.

"I was thinking she might help you, if you asked her."

"Again, I ask, what kind of help do you..." he trailed off. "I see." Arthur moved away from her. "I didn't need your pity fuck, Gwen."

"That is not even in the same universe as the truth."

"Then why do you come here bearing your gifts of Aphrodite's help, if you don't pity me. If you're not trying to put me out of my misery," he snarled.

"I am trying to put you out of your misery because I caused it. All the pain you carry, you don't need that."

"Gwen, I think you should go." He was frozen and stiff, like a statue.

"You don't deserve it," she continued as if he hadn't spoken. "She can make it so you never loved me. All you have to do is ask her."

"This is what you want?"

"It's not about me, Arthur. It's about you."

"No matter what it cost me, I'd never wish away my years with you. Or the time I spent loving you. And if that's what you'd ask of me, then you don't know me at all."

"I just wanted it to be better. I'm giving up something too."

"What? Lance? It sure as hell isn't me and I don't know why I can't get it through my head that you don't want me and you never did." He sat up on the edge of the bed, his back to her.

"I was a stupid child. I'm trying to make it right."

"Just go home, Gwen."

Gwen didn't know what was wrong with her, but all of her guilt had turned to venom. "Just go home? What home? I don't have one. I've never belonged here. I was supposed to die in a monastery repenting my sins. You're always so quick to send me away. You never fought for me. I was just yours. Like some piece of furniture my father handed over to you."

"When did I ever treat you like that? When, Guinevere?" he snarled. "I couldn't court you, I was fighting a war to unite Britain under one flag. When we were building Camelot? When we were teaching our world how to live in peace? I thought you were my partner. I thought you wanted what I wanted."

She realized now that all of her angst was self-made. He'd treated her exactly as she'd wanted, like an equal, not a shrinking maiden and she'd been too blind to see it.

"You wanted me to fight for you?" His voice was softer now. "I thought that's what I was doing when I made you a queen instead of a warlord's lady."

"You were going to let them burn me."

"You must think I'm stupid as well. Of course I knew Lance would save you. If he didn't, I would have killed him myself."

"After I burned."

"Is that really what you think?"

She realized that at the time, it had been. But now? It seemed a traitorous and unworthy thought. "I did."

"I loved you the only way I knew how. I thought that when I didn't set you aside because you didn't give me an heir, that might have made it clear. Maybe I should have told you that I found your special tea that kept you from getting pregnant. That I honored you as my wife and my queen even when I knew you didn't want to be either."

"It always seemed like you were so quick to throw me away." She swallowed. "And I wasn't worthy of the trust you put in me. Or the power you gave me. But I want to change all that. That's why I spoke with Aphrodite. I just want to fix it."

"You can't fix it, Gwen. If you're trying to ease your guilt, just stop. Let it go. You can't change the past, only the future."

"That's what I'm trying to do. I know I can't change the past. But I want to change your future. I want you to be happy." *Because I love you.*

A knock thundered through the heavy wood of the door.

"I'm not to be disturbed," Arthur answered.

"Lancelot awaits you in the solarium," a muffled voice replied.

Gwen was startled to hear his name, but didn't say anything.

"I'm sure he's looking for you. He must have come to his senses." Arthur said quietly, with no judgment in his voice. "You should go to him."

"Again, you're so quick to surrender me even now." She wished he'd just take her in his arms and tell her that he'd never let her go, but again, those were the dreams of a girl. Not a woman grown.

"Must I bleed for you still?" He said raggedly.

"No, you don't have to bleed, but maybe you could ask me to stay instead of pushing me toward a man who doesn't love me."

"I thought when I married you, I wouldn't have to ask again."

"Not then. Now. Ask me to stay." Hope burned wretched and traitorous. This was supposed to be about his feelings, not hers.

"I told you, Gwen. This—" he gestured "—me, this has always been and will always be yours. Choose to stay." Arthur dressed. "I'm going to meet our guest. You're welcome to come with me."

Gwen knew what she wanted to do, she wanted to hide. She didn't want to see Lance. She'd accepted it was over between them, but to be in a room with Arthur and Lance after everything, after so many years, she thought that she might just explode.

Whatever Lance had come here to do, it didn't have anything to do with her.

And yet, if it had to do with Arthur, it did.

She needed to show Arthur that she could be his queen, that it was really what she wanted.

Gwen took her time dressing, not in hopes that Lance would be gone by the time that she was done, but to give them a chance to speak without her between them. Because she'd been a wedge that kept them apart.

She smoothed her hair and her dress and for a moment, she wished she had Morgan's magick to make herself just a little bit presentable.

*This is a one time deal, don't ask again.* Morgan's voice resonated in her head and in that instant, Gwen became a fairy tale princess.

No—she was a queen.

Morgan had outdone herself, dressing her in a white, filmy ball gown and there might have even been glass slippers on her feet.

*Glass. Slippers.*

She caught a glimpse of herself in the beveled mirror that stood in the corner and for the first time in years, Gwen liked what she saw. Not because her ass had gotten any higher or tighter since that last bowl of gelato.

It hadn't.

Not because she looked younger and more radiant.

Even though she did.

But because she finally liked the person who dwelled behind those eyes. She finally liked who she saw looking back at her.

And she finally believed that she was enough. That

gave her the power and the strength to choose to be with Arthur without him taking away culpability or fitting himself into some mold the stories had made for him when the reality of Arthur was a hundred times better.

She exhaled and tried not to cry. It would mess up her magick makeup. "Thanks, Morgan." Gwen said aloud and made her way toward the solarium, but paused when she heard Lance's voice.

"I should have come a long time ago. I'm sorry, Arthur. For everything."

"Are you here as my friend, my brother, my knight? Why now?"

"Because it's time. It's time to own my mistakes and I don't expect you to forgive me."

"Even though you've asked me to?" Arthur's voice was calm and even, no judgment and no anger. He was always good at that, hiding his feelings. Keeping emotion out of his voice. Maybe too good.

"I've learned that I shouldn't ask for forgiveness with the expectation of receiving it. It's kind of like love. You don't love because you expect it in return. You love because you must."

"And I love you, Lance. As I always have. As I always will," Arthur replied.

A weight dropped from Gwen's chest that she didn't know she carried. She was reminded of his behavior when she was talking to Morgan earlier. Lance said if they were making out, he wanted to watch.

Gwen chose that moment to make her entrance and toss his own words back at him. "It's too quiet in here. If you're making out, I get to watch," she teased.

Her eyes met Arthur's and it was as if Lance wasn't even

in the room. There was nothing so bright or glorious as the king standing before her.

"My lady." Arthur bowed.

She held out her hand and he kissed it, the contact sending delicious shivers down her spine.

"You may have whatever you wish. You always could."

She saw that now. "It's good to be queen." Gwen turned to Lance. "I'm glad you came. I'll leave you two alone so that you can talk. I think everything is as it should be."

Lance bowed, a perfect knight. And she realized he was wearing his armor. It gleamed in the light. They'd made each other both more and less than they were meant to be.

"Almost as it should be. I have to see a wicked witch about a thing." He smiled, and it was the smile that Gwen had fallen in love with so many years ago. He was a knight in shining armor again, a man with vows and purpose. The warmth that bloomed in her heart was happiness for him. That he'd found his way.

"Well, that's never going to work." Gwen reached out and marred the shine on the breastplate of his armor. "A man in shining armor is a man who has never been tested. You need some dirt and dings. Then Morgan will take you seriously."

"I'm happy for you, Gwen. I'm happy for us," Lance said.

She looked at Arthur. "Me too."

"All I can say is family dinners are going to be weird." Lance said as he took his leave.

"He's right, you know." Arthur said when he was gone. "He's going to declare himself to my son's mother. Your ex-husband is going to be at every holiday meal from now until eternity." Arthur's mouth curved in a smile.

Gwen giggled. "Your son who killed you and destroyed your kingdom."

"At least it wasn't the Porsche." Arthur shrugged.

"I think to celebrate, you should take me back to bed."

"Is that your first act as queen?"

"No, my first act as queen is to tell you that I love you. Now, take me to bed."

"Yes, Your Highness."

## CHAPTER
# TWENTY-EIGHT

MORGAN

Morgan soothed her sorrows by wandering in the famous orchard of Avalon. She took great joy in her new powers and it made her happy to bring blooms to the trees, green to the grass and see to the health of all the living things on the island.

She'd been happy to supply Gwen with a dress that fit her happily ever after. It was how things were supposed to be.

If only Lance could feel the same way about her that Arthur felt about Guinevere.

She was glad to know that he'd asked Arthur's forgiveness and everything was sliding into place. All it had taken was a visit from Aphrodite to shake up their little burg. Even though things hadn't worked out exactly as she wanted, Morgan was still glad that they'd happened.

Not just because she was Lady of the Lake, but because they'd all been stagnant too long. All living things must grow or die and that's what they'd been doing—all of them

—slowly dying inside while holding on to old dreams and old hurts. It was time to move forward.

Morgan just had to figure out how.

"So, I'm pretty sure I feel your hand in this, Mother."

She looked up to see Mordred standing in front of her, his shadow blocking out the rays of the sun.

"My hand in what, my son?"

"Artemis."

"Yes, of course." Morgan offered him a smile. "Did you learn anything?"

"You knew I would."

"Correction. I *hoped* you would."

"Did you know it would hurt like this?" His tone wasn't harsh or angry, it was clinical. Curious.

"Like what?" Morgan reached out for him, but he declined to embrace her.

"Like fireworks exploding in my chest and burning up all of my blood."

Did she know, he'd asked her. At the time she'd agreed to put Artemis in his way, she'd thought she knew, but she didn't. Not really. She was honest with him. "No, I didn't."

"But you thought it was for the best, right?"

"Of course. I don't wish pain on you, but it's a lesson we must all learn."

"Even you?" He cocked his head to the side.

She handed him a dark red apple. "Especially me."

He eyed the apple, turned it this way and that. "Very wicked witch of you."

"I know. I am what I am. Just as you are what you are," Morgan reassured him.

"I love her." He looked up at her, amethyst eyes dark pools. "I don't mind the pain. I kind of like it, I think."

"Did you tell her?"

"Yes. Stupid girl wanted to break the curse." He acted as if this were the most awful thing she could ever say.

"Why is that stupid? Maybe she wanted to be loved for herself and not because you were cursed."

"We both know that wouldn't happen." Mordred rolled his eyes.

Morgan was amused by her son's utter arrogance. It had been making togas, dresses, and panties fall off of the supernatural female population since he'd come of age. She'd already learned her lessons about arrogance and pride—they were hard ones, but necessary. "Why not? Are you so far removed from the human experience you don't think you can feel love?"

"Is that the lesson?" Mordred asked.

"Maybe." Morgan couldn't tell him what his lessons were, that was for him to figure out. Although, it warmed her heart that he'd asked her. He hadn't come to her for advice in a long time.

"What, are you the Lady of the Lake now to speak in riddles?" he scoffed.

"Yes, I am."

"Excuse me, what?" Her son cocked his head to the side, confused.

"Yes, you heard me. I'm the Lady of the Lake, but I'm not speaking in riddles to confuse you. I just don't know what the lesson is."

"It was Vivienne who cursed me. If she's no longer Lady of the Lake, her curse should be broken." He eyed her warily. "Did you curse me again?"

Morgan could see the direction of his thoughts and offered him a smile. "No, my son."

"But I still love her. It still burns."

"So the love you feel for her is all your own," she prompted.

"That can't be." Disbelief etched itself on his sharp features.

"It can. But I think she's leaving the island."

"It's best." He seemed decisive.

"As you say." She shrugged.

"You're not going to tell me to go after her?"

Mordred seemed to think she was trying to trick him somehow. Oh, how she loved that boy.

"Why should I? You'll do as you wish. You always have."

"You're not very motherly."

"Yes, I am. I meddle in your life plenty." If only he knew...

"I said motherly, not meddlesome." His eyebrows drew together sharply.

"Same difference." She shrugged again.

"You know, I don't enjoy the way you slip in and out of this Lady of the Lake pomposity and your regular self." His left eyebrow had arched in disapproval.

"I'll try to work on that."

"See that you do."

It was the closest thing Mordred came to affection. Except then he surprised her. He asked her, "Why did you call me Little Prince when I was young?"

"Because that's what you are." Morgan eyed him. What an odd question.

"Because of Arthur or because of you?"

She arched a brow in wicked witch fashion. "Because of me, of course. How could you ever think otherwise? You were Avalon born. Magick is your birthright. You are my son and a prince."

"Hmm. And here Artemis thought you'd called me your

little crabapple or something equally and obnoxiously precocious."

"Oh, I did. But you didn't care for it at all. When you were four, you told me to stop calling you inanities and use your name." She remembered it so clearly, as if it had happened yesterday. She'd instructed him to come to her because wanted a hug and he'd acted so insulted at the endearment, for indeed, he had been her little crabapple.

"Four?" His expression was very much like her wicked witching.

"You cried when I held you, enjoyed your own company much more than mine, until you were old enough that I could teach you magick. Then you sat quietly at my work table, cataloguing potions and ingredients. It was the only thing that would hold your attention."

"Was I born bad?" A wistful look crossed his face.

"Don't you remember this part of your lesson?" If he'd forgotten, she might have to rattle his teeth. A smiting was brewing because Morgan had fought long and hard to raise Mordred to do what he must, but not to hate himself.

"About the darkness and the stars? Yes. But that doesn't mean I wasn't born bad."

"No, you weren't born bad. You were born to be who you are. Good or bad, that's always been your choice."

"I'm glad you're my mother," he said thoughtfully.

"I'm glad you're my son." And she was. He'd been a trial, but she'd learned in her long years that all children were—as were all parents.

"Really?"

"Of course, really. What did I teach you about the truth?"

"To always use it because it's the sharpest weapon," he recited dutifully.

"Exactly. I've never lied to you and I never will."

"Do you think that perhaps Artemis would let me love her? If I asked nicely."

"She doesn't get to choose that and neither do you."

Mordred put his hands up over his eyes. "I think this is my cue to make my exit. The shining armor coming over that hill is blinding me. And making me throw up in my mouth."

Morgan knew without looking that it was Lance, but she didn't understand what he was doing. She didn't dare let herself have hope.

"Off with you then. Go catch your goddess before she leaves. Aeron pissed off Aphrodite good and proper, so they're both getting ready to go back to Olympus."

"Aeron, hmm?"

Morgan could see his wheels turning and the fire of inspiration flare. But she didn't say anything to him about being kind, or not interfering. He was who he was and Artemis would either love him for that or she wouldn't. Mordred could hold his own against the god, if he chose to lock horns with him.

The glare from Lancelot's armor blinded her as well and she didn't even see Mordred leave.

"What exactly are you doing?" Morgan asked him in her best Lady of the Lake voice.

"Owning my shit, apologizing, and depending on how that goes, getting the happily ever after I don't deserve," he said.

"I really wish you could turn that shine down on the armor."

"Sorry, can't do it. Gwen tried."

Morgan didn't feel the familiar prickle of irritation at

the mention of the other woman's name. "Do you mean that literally or figuratively?"

"Any tarnishing is on me. Gwen told me that you'd be more inclined toward something a bit more battle-scarred. But it's enchanted."

"Oh, I can fix that." Not that she wanted him to be vulnerable, but she would like to look at his face, rather than that spot of silver that reflected only the sun. When Morgan removed the enchantment, she saw how right he was.

His armor was tarnished, dented, cracked in places, but those cracks were like wounds and they healed as she watched.

The armor was very much like Lance himself.

"Is that better?" he asked.

"Much, much better." She didn't dare to hope, and yet, a small seed in her heart flowered anyway.

He drew his sword and sank to one knee, palm atop the pommel.

This was the Lance she'd fallen in love with, the shining armor had always just been packaging.

"First I must ask your forgiveness for my selfishness and my cruelty."

"Lance—" She was going to say that she understood and there was never anything to forgive.

"I spoke with Vivienne and I've misunderstood everything for so long. I've been so worried about being what everyone wanted me to be that I became everything *I* didn't want to be. I thought I'd lived in service to something greater my whole life, but I didn't. I lived in service to myself. So I've come to ask to change that. I want to live in service to you. I offer you my sword, Morgan, Lady of the Lake."

His words were like a punch in the face. She'd gone numb and she didn't know what to say.

"And as unworthy as it is, I offer you my heart too. Let me be your Champion, your personal guard, anything. Just forgive me and let me be with you."

"This isn't what you want." She'd give him just one chance to take it back.

"Oh, yes it is." He looked up, and the intensity in his eyes was brighter than the armor. It seared her to the very marrow of her bones. "Remember when I asked you to use me, Morgan? Use me until we'd left nothing undone? There's still much yet for us to explore."

"I don't understand." But her mouth had gone dry at the mention of everything they'd left unexplored, undone. She was reminded of heat, the way his flesh burned into hers and the way his every touch ignited something dangerous inside of her.

"I didn't understand at first either. You're so strong, Morgan. You don't need anyone. I wasn't man enough to accept your strength, to not be needed."

The numbness fled and Morgan melted. "Oh, Lance. I need you. How could you ever think I didn't?"

"Vivienne said you don't." He paused. "But she said you wanted me and that was so much better."

"And is it better?" She bit her lip. "Because once I accept your service, Lance, I will never release you. So you better be sure. I'm not like Gwen. She just wants you to be happy and I just want you to be mine."

"Still wicked witching?" The corner of his mouth turned up in a smirk. "I already agreed to *that* kind of magick. How many ways do I have to say it? I love you, Morgan."

Another punch in the face, but in a good way. "I love you, too." She held her breath for just a second to keep that moment in time from moving forward. She wanted to savor it for as long as she could. "This is your last chance to change your mind." She closed her eyes because she didn't want to see any doubt cross his face.

Instead, his lips crashed into hers, hot and demanding. In this case, Morgan Le Fey had no problem with surrender.

# TWENTY-NINE

APHRODITE

"I want to go home," Artemis said in a rush when she bolted through the door of Aphrodite's room.

Aphrodite was glad to hear it. "I'm ready to go too. This vacation wasn't anything like what I'd expected or hoped for."

"Me either."

"I'm sorry, I feel like it's my fault." Aphrodite pulled Artemis in for a hug.

Only, when she hugged her, Aphrodite sensed the blooming of new love.

And she knew that they couldn't leave. Not yet.

She owed it to Artemis to let her—make her—realize that the bad boy would make a good man. Aphrodite could feel it in the air.

A sort of electric buzz vibrated around them and Aphrodite sighed. "I think we're going to have wait a few minutes."

"Why? Let's go now. Right now."

"Your dark horse is coming. And you need to listen to what he has to say."

"I—" Artemis looked like a centaur caught in a pair of bright headlights. "No."

"Yes," Aphrodite said gently. "For me."

"For you, or for Love?"

"Same thing."

Artemis huffed. "Fine." She flopped on the bed. "But I don't know what else there is to say."

"Less talking, Artemis, and more listening. Really listen to him. Not only his words, but what's beneath them." When it came to matters of the heart, Aphrodite felt like all of the people of the world were her children and she was the wise mama. Which meant it was probably pretty pathetic that she couldn't handle her own business.

Or maybe she had after all. This thing with Aeron was lust, not love. He was the one who was in danger of falling. Not her. And while she could tweak lust, it was love that was really her realm. So, she actually had nothing to be embarrassed about.

She'd even broken it off with Ares and meant it, so maybe things weren't so bleak after all.

"Are we there yet?" Artemis huffed.

"Do you see tall, pale and broody anywhere? No? Then obviously we're not there yet."

"I don't know why I let you talk me into this." Artemis started pacing. "This was all such a bad idea. All I wanted to do was have someone completely unsuitable relieve me of the V-Card. I didn't want to fall in love."

"Okay, let's think about this for a minute. Did you really think, no really, that you could come to a beach resort with the Goddess of Love and not have some mad, passionate affair?" Aphrodite eyed her as if she were dumber than a goat.

"I should have known when you took me out for pizza and baked a cake. I should have known." Artemis crossed her arms over her chest.

"I just want you to be happy, Artie."

Artemis rewarded her with a tiny smile. "Mordred said that Artie is a fat garbage man from Omaha, not the Goddess of the Hunt."

"I don't care what he's sticking where, I'll call you whatever I like. You were my friend before you were his girl."

Artemis laughed. "You're assuming quite a bit."

"Yeah, after millennia, you should know Love is like that."

"Can't you go pester Demeter?"

"She and Eros are still on vacation. And you know, he's never taken one. Ever. So I'm not going to disturb them."

"Confess. Once you found out he loved her, did you work your gris-gris on her?"

"Of course not. It happened all on its own."

"If it hadn't, would you have?"

Aphrodite flashed a sly smile. "He's my son. I'd do anything to make him happy. But I'll tell you a secret. I knew when Hades begged me to pull his heart out of his chest that it would weave a new tapestry, one where everyone, including Hades got their happily ever after. I had a little help from Fate, but I did actually know what I was doing."

Artemis exhaled heavily and started drumming her fingers on the table. "If he's not here in five minutes, I'm leaving. The prey doesn't wait for the predator. That's just stupid."

"So that means you'd rather scurry back to Olympus like a scared rabbit? That's not like you, Artie."

"Artie is a fat garbage man in Omaha, I already told you." Mordred stood in the door, carrying a small cage that had been packed full of what looked like a baby dragon. "Sorry it took me a minute. I had to stop and pick this up for you, Aphrodite."

"I don't understand." Aphrodite accepted the cage.

"I'm not without my talents." Mordred winked at her and led Artemis outside.

Aphrodite set the cage up on the table and eyed the creature. "Aren't you just adorable?"

"No, I'm not adorable. I'm trapped. And I'm going to smite the shit out of Mordred when I get out of here," Aeron's voice echoed from the cage.

Aphrodite couldn't fight the smirk on her face. She kind of didn't want to. "How did he get you in there?"

"Magick, obviously." Her snorted again. "A little help, here?"

"Only if you promise to wait to smite Mordred until after he's had his say with Artemis."

"Not a chance."

"I guess that's my answer too."

"You can't be serious."

"As the Kraken." No way was she letting handsome here ruin Artemis's moment.

"Damn it. Fine."

"Fine, *what*? I need to hear it. Specifics." She knew better than to leave any ambiguities when dealing with gods.

"I will wait to smite Mordred until he's had his say with Artemis." He huffed and snorted, little puffs of smoke still billowing out of his snout. "Well, what are you waiting for?"

"It's just, you're so cute."

"I didn't do this to you when you were pink and face down in the sand."

"No, but maybe you're nicer than I am?" Aphrodite grinned, but she reached out and opened the cage. When she did, Aeron took his humanoid shape.

And he was naked.

"You need to put a leash on that thing."

"You said you wanted the dragon. Here he is."

Aphrodite rolled her eyes. "Do you know how many times I've heard something similar from Ares? Do you guys get together and write down stuff like this to whip it out later, because if so, you should scrap everything and start over with new material."

"That's not what you were saying earlier."

She rolled her eyes again. "Earlier you hadn't accused me of trying to take over your island for my own nefarious ends."

Aeron manifested his yummy gladiator costume and Aphrodite tried really hard not to look, but really, one could only expect so much from a girl. Even a goddess.

"I'll admit, I may owe you an apology. Speaking strategically—"

Aphrodite make mock-talking motions with her hands. "I'll tell you what you can do with your *strategically*."

"If it involves any orifices, I think you can keep it to yourself."

"That's exactly what I'm saying. I don't want to hear your excuses."

"Oh. I see what you did there."

"Good. Because if it was lost on you, you'd be slower than a box of turtles."

"Are you still pissed I wouldn't sleep with you?"

"No, and I was never pissed. Just thwarted. Surprised." She shrugged. "Definitely surprised, but I saw where you were coming from. It's not a big deal. You were right." She turned away from him and fiddled with her suitcase.

"Are you leaving?"

"Yeah. Vacation didn't turn out to be very relaxing for either one of us, so we're going home."

"It would be a shame that you came all this way and didn't have a good time."

"All this way? We travel at the speed of thought."

"Yes, but we have an image to maintain. Is there anything I can do to change your mind about leaving?" His expression was earnest.

"No. Not so much. But I won't tell anyone I had a horrible time. It wasn't Avalon's fault. It was my own."

"Do you think they're done yet?" His nodded toward the door.

"No. Most assuredly not. Maybe you could just go on and do whatever it is you do and leave them alone. You can smite Mordred tomorrow. It's not like he's going anywhere."

Aeron smiled at her. "I really do like you, Aphrodite."

"I liked you more than I should."

"Liked? As in, past tense?" He arched a brow.

"Well, you know. It'd never work out, anyway."

"You don't have to throw the battle ax out with the warlord. I'd hoped we could just slow down and start with dinner."

"I don't know. You might get all tactical on me and then where would we be?" she teased.

"You're right." He shrugged. "But it could be fun."

"So, let me get this straight. Are we friends or is this a date?"

"Can we figure that out later?" He shrugged.

"I think we need to make another deal." He was so mellow and laid back, she almost didn't know what to do with herself.

"You're as bad as I am with the treaties and tactics. Don't even act like you're not."

"No, I wouldn't lie." It was Aphrodite's turn to smirk. "I think you should promise me that you're never going to smite Mordred for today. Without him, we wouldn't have spoken again."

"I'm sure in all of eternity we might have run into each other."

"I don't think so. It took this long for a first sighting."

"I'm only agreeing because you agreed to dinner."

She technically hadn't, but that was okay. Aphrodite could give him this one. "I'll probably need a date for the wedding."

"Who's getting married?"

"It'll probably be more like a handfasting. Morgan and Lance, Gwen and Arthur, Vivienne and Hector, it'll be a free for all. A job well done, I say."

"Are we still negotiating? Because I'm not wearing a suit."

"No one asked you to. In fact, that little number you have on right now will be fine." Her gaze traveled down his body and back up again.

"I think that's my line."

"Toh-may-to, toh-mah-to." She grinned.

Things really had turned out for the best. If she'd shagged Aeron, it would've been fun for all of—she eyed him again—however long he could keep up with her, but it wouldn't have fixed her heart. She was still healing from Ares and she didn't know how long that was going to take.

But she had eternity and Aeron was willing to take it slow. She liked that about him. Well, not initially, she'd never had a man say no before, but after she'd thought about it, she liked that there were things more important to him than poon and war hammers.

This wasn't how she expected her vacation to end, but it might've been the best one yet.

# THIRTY

ARTEMIS

S he didn't want to look at him.

Mordred being there, it was everything she wanted and everything she feared. She should've known Aphrodite would do her damndest to make sure Artemis got True Love, with the capital letters, for her birthday rather than just a shag.

With Mordred Le Fey, no less.

Of course, he couldn't be gallant and let her get away with it.

"You won't even look at me?" he said.

"It hurts to look at you. No man should be as beautiful as you are."

"Thank you." She could hear the smirk in his voice. "You can tell me that whenever you like."

"I'm sure you've had plenty of women tell you that."

"I have," he agreed easily. "But they weren't you."

"What are you doing?" Artemis cried.

"Trying to get you to at least look at me when I make my grand confession. It's rather insulting that you won't."

"That's not—you know what I mean. Didn't we beat this to death already?"

"Not quite."

"Fine. We'll do this like a Band-Aid. Just rip it off so it can start healing." She looked up at him and she was struck again by the sheer beauty of him.

Which made it worse. Artemis had seen all of the wrong done by beautiful men. It was rare that they gave anyone a Happily Ever After but themselves. Women like her ended up alone and brokenhearted after falling for their stupid lines. Artemis knew she was just a conquest. How could she not be? It was because she'd said no, which presented a challenge. He'd tire of her all too quickly after the curse was broken.

She loved the chase more than anyone, after all. Artemis knew its allure.

"Artemis, don't you know your own appeal?"

She shrugged. "I've been told I'm beautiful. But it's not about what I look like. Or even what you look like." Even though it kind of was, but she wasn't going to say that. The curse part was still the biggest problem. "It's about what I know you don't really feel."

"Are you me? Have you walked in my skin? Have you had my heart in your chest that you know what it feels and what it doesn't?"

"We both know you're cursed. Let it go, Mordred. This hurts."

"Artemis," he whispered, dipping his head close to her lips. "What hurts is the thought of you leaving. Of never holding you in my arms again, never hearing your laugh. I love you. And not because of some stupid curse. Morgan became Lady of Lake after the first day. The curse was broken then. This is me."

Artemis was almost afraid to believe it. "What about what you said about pain?"

"Apparently, that's just how love feels. It's a strange kind of ache that burns and yearns. I've never experienced anything like this before. And I still don't want it to stop." He suddenly released her.

She felt the loss of his arms, his heat and his strength acutely. Artemis didn't like it.

"But because it's real, part of me wants to remind you of all the reasons you don't or shouldn't want me. Because I know I'm not good enough for you. I know my own failings and I am bad. I destroy, I corrupt."

Artemis's fingers and toes tingled as the bloom inside of her chest spread through her whole body. The curse had been broken and he still loved her.

Aphrodite wouldn't have made her wait if this wasn't real.

And really, it came down to trusting him. Not what Aphrodite said, not the curse, not anything but what was between the two of them.

Artemis didn't know if he was going to hurt her or if she was going to hurt him. She had no idea what the future held and for the most part, she didn't want to know. She wanted to live in the moment.

And in *this* moment, she was filled with an over-whelming love for the man in front of her. A man who dared to bare all his weaknesses, all his flaws, and asked her to love him anyway.

When she still hadn't said anything, he continued. "I wish I could change. But I can't."

"I don't want you to change," she blurted.

"No?"

"No." She shook her head and with her next words, leapt off the proverbial cliff. "I love you just the way you are."

"Thank the Goddess." He dragged her against him.

"Which one?" she teased.

"Aphrodite, I think. I'll have to sacrifice chocolate on her altar later."

"You're my birthday present." Artemis grinned against his chest.

"You're my everything."

And when he kissed her, she knew that he spoke the truth.

# THIRTY-ONE

The First Handfasting

Aphrodite was wrong in her assumption the happy couples would all handfast together. Morgan and Vivienne decided that Gwen and Arthur should be first without sharing the spotlight.

Mostly it was a financial decision. With two of their three main tourist attractions out of order, they'd use the weddings to boost Avalon's economy until they decided what else they could do to draw supernatural vacationers.

The three of them, Gwen, Morgan and Vivienne, decided to draw out each affair. A handfasting, then re-crowning Gwen as queen, lots of pomp, circumstances, and catering. Gwen was more than happy to do her part because it meant Arthur was hers, and hers alone.

Artemis had to admit that she liked the sound of that and Mordred's proposal had come written in the stars. Literally. He and Nyx, her sister-in-law, got along famously and she helped. Apollo still didn't care too much for him,

SARANNA DEWYLDE

but he'd stopped trying to burn his face off and that was saying something.

Morgan and Lance decided on something smaller, more intimate. Sure, they were happy to put on the show, but they'd vowed their troth to each other already among the apple trees in Avalon's famous orchard where they met. And she wore the purple lace dress that had him so entranced.

Vivienne, as much as she loved Hector had reservations about handfasting with a man so many years her junior, but when he asked her for her hand, all she could say was yes.

Aphrodite thought that it was funny how all of these loves simply fell into place once hers fell apart. But she wasn't bitter, and she was so happy for all of her friends. She was even happy for herself. She and Aeron were dating and neither were in a hurry to rush into anything.

They still had to deal with Ares because even though he'd said he wanted Aphrodite to be happy, he was convinced that she'd be happiest with him. Her sincere break up with him had been a kick to the war hammer and he was determined to win her hand. Aeron had encouraged her to let him try, because he could only win if she was still in love with him.

But their adventures aren't over. Ares is loud and determined to be heard, so look for Desperate Housewives of Olympus: ARES coming soon.

# ABOUT THE AUTHOR

Saranna De Wylde has always been fascinated by things better left in the dark. She wrote her first story after watching The Exorcist at a slumber party. Since then, she's published horror, romance and narrative nonfiction. Like all writers, Saranna has held a variety of jobs, from operations supervisor for an airline, to an assistant for a call girl, to a corrections officer. But like Hemingway said, "Once writing has become your major vice and greatest pleasure, only death can stop it." So she traded in her cuffs for a full-time keyboard. She loves to hear from her readers.

Keep up with releases, events and access to special content by signing up the Saranna DeWylde newsletter here: www.corvuscoraxbooks.com

# ALSO BY SARANNA DEWYLDE

Desperate Housewives of Olympus

Desperate Housewives of Olympus: Ares

Other Series:

Margie Majors: Middle-Aged Vampire Slayer

10 Days

Fairy Godmothers Inc.

The Woolven Secret

Saranna also writes as Sara Arden, Sara Wylde, Sara Lunsford, and Sara Ravencroft.

www.ingramcontent.com/pod-product-compliance
Lightning Source LLC
Chambersburg PA
CBHW031025260626
47153CB00017B/2125